The Lamp

Presented To:

_____

From:

_____

Date:

_____

JUST BELIEVE.

JIM STOVALL
WITH
TRACY J TROST

DESTINY IMAGE₀ PUBLISHERS, INC.

P.O. Box 310, Shippensburg, PA 17257-0310

For a U.S. bookstore nearest you, call 1-800-722-6774. For more information on foreign distributors, call 717-532-3040.

Reach us on the Internet: www.destinyimage.com

ISBN 13 TP: 978-0-7684-3785-0
ISBN 13 Ebook: 978-0-7684-8994-1

For Worldwide Distribution, Printed in the U.S.A.
1 2 3 4 5 6 / 14 13 12 11

DEDICATION

This book is dedicated to my colleagues at Trost Moving Pictures, Destiny Image Publishers, and my team at the Narrative Television Network who saw this story not only as a book but as a major motion picture.

It is also dedicated to my friends and family who taught me in word and deed that dreams do come true, regardless of your circumstances—if you just believe.

And, finally, this book is dedicated to Dorothy Thompson who, once again, has taken my dictated words and turned them into the book you hold in your hands.

Our destiny is waiting from our choices.
I am as healthy as I believe myself to be.
I am as wealthy as I believe.
I am only as blessed as I consider myself blessed.
I am as happy as I will allow myself to become blessed.
My life is as productive as I, myself, will permit.

Anyone old enough,
Having failed often enough,
Wept hard enough,
And laughed regularly enough,
Can find a flame of hope enough
For each of us.

FROM THE PERSONAL DIARY OF JOYE KANELAKOS

FOREWORD

I think when we are young we have a tendency to dream big and shoot for the stars. But, at some point along the way, many people lose their extraordinary dreams and become content with ordinary lives—settling into familiar routines and letting life pass by.

On an early July morning in 1969, I was driving along a nearly deserted highway on my way to an insurance sales meeting. It was Friday and I looked forward to finishing my business and then enjoying a weekend with my wife, Shirley. I enjoyed my work, but the weekends were what I really looked forward to. And I could have lived my life for years doing the same thing I was doing that day, over and over again.

But on that early July morning, my life changed forever. I was involved in a devastating automobile accident. Fortunately everyone survived, and even though the accident was not my fault, I faced potentially financially devastating legal issues. This resulting trouble led me, in 1972, to start the company that is now known as Pre-Paid Legal Services, Inc.

In the years following the 1969 accident, my wife and I had several choices to make along the way. We could have allowed the circumstances of life to force me into work that was meaningless and meant only to pay the bills. And believe me, I understand the temptation to settle in and trade time for money. At times it can seem to be the easy way out; so I understand that temptation, but I knew it wasn't for me. That's what this book is about. It's about taking a life, maybe your life, and finding happiness. It's about how to decide that life should be better—that it will be better.

Do you know someone who has just settled into life? Do you know someone who is miserable spending their entire week looking forward to the weekend? Do you know someone for whom the weekend, instead of a fulfilling life, holds the promise of happiness?

If that sounds like you or someone you know, I'm glad you're reading this book. I hope the wisdom shared in the contemporary story you now hold in your hands will enlighten and inspire you. In fact, if you will let it, I believe the principles and practices outlined in this book could quite literally change your life.

I believe in the power of changing lives so much that I've built my company around this very concept.

For decades Pre-Paid Legal has been in the business of providing a revolutionary service through a method that has helped many people, just like you, achieve their dreams. I have heard stories of retail workers leaving their 80-hour workweek drudgery to enjoy lives of fulfillment—to finally be able to pay their bills. I have seen lawyers, doctors, janitors, and teachers change their lives with the opportunity Pre-Paid Legal offers. In fact, at press time, Pre-Paid Legal has welcomed 135 people into the Millionaire Club, meaning that those people have each earned $1 million or more in their careers with Pre-Paid Legal.

But it's not just about the money. Pre-Paid Legal is about making a living while making a difference. While I have witnessed many successes with the business opportunity available through Pre-Paid Legal, I have enjoyed reading countless letters from people who use the service we provide. If you want to see the difference we're making in the lives of people every day, all you have to do is read a few of those letters—we post many of them on our company Website.

Jim Stovall is a dear friend of mine. I am so honored to be involved in your experience with his latest work, The Lamp. It is my deepest wish that you find happiness, that you make decisions that lead to joy and fulfillment, and that somehow you and those you love will be enriched and blessed by the message of this book.

You'll have to read the book to understand my closing remark, but this may very well be your "Charles" moment. The decision is yours to make.

Best wishes for the life you want and deserve.

HARLAND C. STONECIPHER, Founder
Pre-Paid Legal Services, Inc.

INTRODUCTION

The Lamp has become a very special story to me.

In 1996, a good friend who is a Broadway producer and event promoter contacted me and asked if I would be interested in doing an arena speaking tour featuring Og Mandino and me. As an author myself, I was ecstatic at the prospect of working with one of the greatest writers of our time; and as a speaker, the thought of getting to do an arena tour with Og Mandino was very compelling.

A few weeks before our first event was scheduled, the promoter called me and said, "We have a slight problem." When I asked him to elaborate, he told me that Og Mandino had died the night before. I informed the promoter that if that is a slight problem, I didn't want to be around if there was a major problem.

I told the promoter to simply cancel the tour, but he challenged me with an amazing question. He asked what I would do if I had an arena full of people and I wanted to impact their lives.

Since the promoter worked predominantly with Broadway events and entertainment projects, I let my mind wander and told him that I would like to create a two-and-a-half hour event with an intermission, just like a Broadway show.

We created music, laser images, and big screen interviews with children telling what they wanted to do when they grew up, as well as 100-year-old people explaining what was important in their lives. The show was entitled *Discover Your Destiny*.

I was really excited about each element of the show, but something was missing. I decided to write a brief one-act play that my friend and colleague Kelly Morrison and I would perform together. That's exactly what we did.

The play was entitled *The Lamp* and was a very popular part of the *Discover Your Destiny* show. Years later, I was contacted by a publisher, and it became a book.

Then my friend and movie partner Tracy J. Trost and I started thinking about *The Lamp* as a movie. As we turned the story into a feature film, I adapted what I had previously written into the book you hold in your hands.

Ironically, the publisher of this book and the distributor of the film are my friends at Destiny who share its name with the long-ago show I created, *Discover Your Destiny*, which was the genesis of *The Lamp*.

The idea of a magic lamp and three wishes is as old as the written or spoken word, but I hope in this modern adaptation you and your family will find new hopes, dreams, and ambitions in which you can just believe.

After you read this book, be sure to check out the movie of *The Lamp* starring Academy Award-winner Louis Gossett Jr., Jason London, Meredith Salinger, Muse Watson, and an ensemble cast of gifted and committed actors.

It is truly a joy for me to experience my written words come to life on a movie screen. Even though a number of my books have been turned into movies, it is always a humbling and gratifying dream-come-true for me.

You may have seen movies based on other novels of mine such as *The Ultimate Gift*, *The Ultimate Life*, or *A Christmas Snow*. If so, you may remember that I had a brief cameo in each film as the limo driver. Somehow I enjoy the image of a blind guy driving a limo. If you've seen all my movies, or if *The Lamp* is your first, I think you will enjoy my feeble acting efforts as a chauffeur.

You would not be the first person to wonder about the oddity of a blind person being in the movie business. It actually comes naturally to me as, for the past 20 years, my company—the Emmy Award-winning Narrative Television Network—has made movies and television accessible to the 13 million blind and visually impaired Americans and millions more around the world.

If you would like to experience this yourself or share it with a visually impaired friend or loved one, just pick up the DVD of *The Lamp* movie and select the narration setting on the menu.

A dear friend of mine once said, "If you can tell a great story, you earn the right to share your message." I hope in these pages you experience a great story and a powerful message; but what's more, I hope you and your family can take this message and bring it to life in your own world.

Several years ago, Barbara Eden was starring in a Broadway show adapted from Neil Simon's play *The Odd Couple*. I attended the show and went backstage afterward to meet Barbara. We sat and talked for a long time. Barbara Eden is known around the world for playing a magic genie in the television show *I Dream of Jeannie*. I quickly forgot about the fact that she was a beautiful movie and television star, and our conversation dealt mostly with wishes, hopes, and dreams.

I think the magic that involves a genie and a lamp begins and ends with you and me thinking about what is possible instead of what is practical. It is easy to live our lives focusing on why things can't happen, but every once in a while, it's good to ask, "What if?" and just believe.

JIM STOVALL

2011

CHAPTER 1

Every day dawns filled with promise, potential, and possibility.

Lisa Walters had not experienced those feelings at the beginning of a new day for several years. She was jolted awake from a deep sleep by the rude and abrupt intrusion of the alarm clock on her bedside table. She groaned, rolled over, and glanced at the offending clock. Lisa was incredulous to discover that it was already 7:00 A.M.. She would have sworn that she had just lain down; and as she slapped the alarm clock into silence, Lisa realized that she was more tired than she had been the night before when she went to bed.

As had become her custom, she glanced at the other side of the bed which, once again, revealed that it had not been slept in, and Lisa knew she was still alone in every way.

As Lisa rolled out of her warm bed, more from habit than anything else, she knew that the best part of her day was already over. Going to sleep each night seemed to be her only respite from the impossible life she was living. A dreamless sleep, or even a nightmare, seemed better than the reality that confronted her every day.

Lisa began the mindless routine of going through her morning ritual which involved getting ready for another day. She showered and dressed without thinking or even being aware of her surroundings. She gave her image one last glance in the mirror and wondered how everything that had started out so right could have possibly gone so wrong.

As she had no answer to this daily question, she stumbled out of the bedroom and down the hallway.

Lisa paused and glanced into her son Eddy's bedroom where she saw her husband, Stanley, once again sleeping in Eddy's single bed. He had obviously slept fitfully and was tangled in Eddy's rumpled comforter that was covered with a baseball player design.

The walls were filled with posters of baseball players. On the dresser were Little League team photos and several baseball trophies. Lisa's eye stopped on the photo of her son, Eddy, wearing his baseball uniform and smiling at the camera. Another photo showed Eddy and his teammates posed for a team picture with Stanley smiling proudly, standing behind the players. Stanley was wearing a baseball cap and his coach's whistle.

Lisa remembered those times as if they were yesterday, but when she tried to capture the feelings, they seemed like ancient history.

Lisa's gaze slid toward the familiar sight of a photo from Eddy's last birthday party. Friends and family were gathered around a brightly lit birthday cake with the number 7 written in icing. The seven represented the number on Eddy's baseball uniform and the fact that they were celebrating his seventh birthday.

Just when she thought she couldn't feel any more empty and desolate, Lisa's memory drifted back to Eddy's funeral just a few weeks after that final birthday party.

It was a cold, rainy day that mirrored Lisa's mood during the funeral and seemed to set the tone for what she feared would be the rest of her life. There was a somber group of friends and family gathered around the small casket at the graveside.

Lisa pondered how few things in life evoke greater sorrow than the image of a casket. Ironically, she thought that the smaller the casket, the greater the sorrow.

Lisa knew that the minister had said some words that were intended to be comforting, but she couldn't hear them on that fateful day, and any intended comfort fell on deaf ears, then and now.

As Lisa looked back at the baseball team photo with Stanley's smiling image, she tried to recapture that moment, but failed once again. That same photo had been displayed among the flower arrangements on Eddy's casket.

As she recalled the funeral scene, the one image seared into her memory was Stanley's angry face staring off into the distance. It didn't even seem like the same person who was the proud baseball coach smiling at her from the team photo.

Stanley couldn't focus on anyone or anything at Eddy's funeral. That faraway gaze and angry countenance seemed to be a permanent fixture in Stanley's life. He stood at the gravesite like a statue as all of the mourners quietly and respectfully drifted away. He didn't or wouldn't hear the murmured condolences and words of encouragement from friends and family.

There was one lone figure who had been standing a distance from the graveside service. It was an older man whose face was shrouded in sadness. No one noticed him, even though he was the last one to leave the cemetery on the day of Eddy's funeral.

Lisa took one last look into her son's bedroom. The posters, photos, and memorabilia of her son's joyous but short life seemed to be mocked and defiled by the sight of Stanley lying in Eddy's bed. Lisa would never be able to pass this room without seeing the image of Stanley seated on that bed holding his son's baseball glove and crying into it the day after the funeral. That scene played over and over in Lisa's mind like a perverse and persistent film loop that just wouldn't stop.

Lisa sighed as she walked away from Eddy's bedroom door and all the memories left inside, along with her sleeping husband who had become more distant than a stranger.

At the end of the hallway, Lisa entered the living room. Even though she had tried to rearrange the furniture and décor several times, she was always struck by the memory of the friends and family who gathered for the reception right after Eddy's funeral service.

The room had been filled with their friends and family who were all trying to think of something to say that mattered. Stanley wouldn't talk to anyone or even come into the house. He just stood on the front porch with that same angry stare.

At least Lisa had been able to feel the loss and sorrow, but Stanley only felt guilt and an all-consuming anger.

As Lisa walked out of the front door, crossed the porch, and descended the steps toward the front walk, she looked at the driveway where her whole world had changed just two years ago.

CHAPTER 2

Stanley—filled with pride, joy, and expectation—placed a bicycle helmet on his son, Eddy. Eddy sat triumphantly on his bike that had just had the training wheels removed for the first time. Stanley held the training wheels in his hand and thought that this was one of the true rites of passage in a young boy's life.

Stanley beamed as he watched his son riding his bike for the first time without training wheels. Eddy was a picture in focus and concentration as he shakily piloted the bicycle down the driveway.

Stanley called, "Be careful, son."

Eddy's laughter could be heard fading into the distance as Stanley's dream, once again, abruptly ended. He awoke, as usual, in his son's bed lamenting the fact that he seemed to be doomed to reliving the last great moment in his life just before he awoke each morning and was faced with the reality of a cold, cruel, and unforgiving world.

Stanley sat up and gazed around his son's room that displayed all of the familiar mementos that proved how much his life had changed.

From the angle of the sun's rays slanting through Eddy's window, Stanley could tell that it was late in the morning. He grumbled and got to his feet, thinking how he used to be a morning person who enjoyed the beginning of each new day; but that was when joy and excitement had been part of his world.

As he stumbled out of Eddy's room, the clock showed that it was 10 o'clock, and Stanley realized he was still wearing his clothes from the day before. He rubbed his face and thought there was a time in his life when things like that had mattered.

It was only a few steps down the hallway to the home office. Stanley rounded the corner and walked through the door to what used to be a productive place filled with energy. Now it seemed like a museum of memories that paid tribute to a long gone time that could never be recaptured.

There were several pictures on the wall of Eddy playing baseball with his teammates. Stanley had been proud to be their coach and had wanted those photos around him as it was such an important part of his life, but that had been then.

The bookshelves were filled with more baseball memorabilia and several technical manuals that bore the author's name *Stanley Walters*.

Stanley had never wanted to do anything for a career other than be a writer. He remembered the pride and promise he had felt when he held one of those newly published books in his hands for the first time. Now they lined up on the shelf like a firing squad that looked menacingly down on him as he sat at his desk and stared at a blank computer screen.

Stanley remembered the days when he would get into a creative flow, and the words seemed to effortlessly appear on the page. Back then, he couldn't imagine a time when he wouldn't or couldn't write.

Stanley glanced at the answering machine on his desk and saw the light blinking. He knew that no one would be calling him with good news. Stanley sighed and braced himself as he pushed the button on the machine and heard the first message.

"This message is for Stanley Walters. This is Melinda with World Card Visa. Your payment on the Visa ending in 0516 is now 120 days past due. Please contact our offi…"

Stanley had heard enough, and he pushed the button to listen to the next message.

"Mr. Walters, this is Steve with Allied Collections again about your overdue mortgage payment. We didn't get the check you promised. If we don't get something soon, we are going to be forced to…"

Stanley thought, *Same song, different verse* as he hit the button once again.

He heard a familiar voice say, "Stan, this is Joel. You remember, your publisher? Hey, man, I need to hear from you right away. I can't get you any more extensions. If I don't get your pages by the end of the month, I am going to need to get that advance back. Don't make me do that. Just call me."

Stanley sat silently and stared at the blank computer screen before him. His dog, Cooper, entered the room and sat at Stanley's feet and stared up into his face.

Cooper was a pit bull/lab mix with sprinklings of many other breeds. He carried himself with dignity and intelligence, seeming to pull the best from every branch of his heritage. Cooper stared at Stanley as if he wanted to help, but somehow he knew that what Stanley needed most was a silent, understanding, and forgiving companion.

After what could have been a few minutes or a few hours, Stanley got up and began to walk aimlessly down the hallway and out the front door. Stanley had no idea where he was going or why he was walking. Cooper matched his stride confidently as he knew exactly where Stanley was going.

Stanley plodded down the picturesque, tree-lined street with Cooper trotting alongside. Moving into this neighborhood had been a great source of pride and joy for

Stanley just a few short years ago, but now he might as well have been living in a desert. All of the sights, scenes, and precious memories ceased to be part of Stanley's life on a fateful day two years before.

Without thinking about where he was going or why he was going there, Stanley rounded the corner at the end of the block and approached a neighborhood park where the Little League baseball diamond was located. Cooper bounded ahead confidently, knowing their destination was in sight, as Stanley walked along in a trance, oblivious of the sights and sounds of the park and the local youth team, The Tigers, practicing on the field.

Sam, the elderly groundskeeper for the park, noticed Stanley and Cooper approaching. Sam immediately recognized Stanley from Eddy's funeral. Even though Sam had been standing some distance away from the gravesite, he instantly recognized Stanley and the expression of bitterness and anger on his face.

CHAPTER 3

The Tigers, the local youth baseball team, were practicing on the field in the neighborhood park. Sam, the groundskeeper, always liked to watch the kids practice, so he arranged his schedule of duties so that he would be cleaning a tractor at the edge of the field during the practice.

Out of the corner of his eye, Sam continued to watch Stanley and Cooper approaching, and he looked on as they sat down in the bleachers.

Sam ambled over to where Stanley and Cooper were sitting and watching the kids on the field. Sam called a greeting. "Hey, there."

Stanley turned his head toward Sam and nodded without expression.

Sam continued. "Which one is yours?"

"Huh?" Stanley seemed confused.

Sam pointed toward the field by way of explanation and said, "Kid. Which one is yours?"

Stanley grimaced and mumbled, "None, actually. I don't have any children."

Sam nodded as if everything was starting to make sense and uttered, "Ah."

Stanley continued to stare blankly toward the kids playing baseball. As the silence stretched out, Sam became uncomfortable.

Finally, Sam offered, "My name is Sam."

Stanley muttered, "Uh-huh."

Sam was undaunted and pointed toward Cooper, asking, "And who is this fine specimen?"

Stanley was starting to be annoyed by Sam. He glared toward him, then glanced down at Cooper, and resumed watching the baseball practice.

Finally, realizing Sam wasn't going to leave, Stanley said, "Cooper."

Sam reached down to pet Cooper, but Cooper immediately extended his paw to shake. Sam chuckled and shook Cooper's paw.

Sam bowed slightly and said, "Well, hello, Cooper. Pleased to make your acquaintance."

Cooper wagged his tail in response.

Stanley, Cooper, and Sam all stared silently at the field for several moments.

Finally, Stanley blurted, "That coach is worthless."

Sam inquired, "How do you mean?"

Stanley explained, "That pitcher has got an arm, but he is throwing all wrong. A good coach would catch that."

Sam chuckled and said, "That's Josh... She can throw the ball all right."

Just then the catcher pulled off his mask and ran out to the mound to talk to the pitcher. As they both removed their caps, the pitcher's long hair fell down around her shoulders.

Stanley nodded with understanding and said, "Oh, I see."

Sam added, "Yeah, Josh is a great kid. I believe she is one of Miss Esther's kids."

Stanley followed Sam's gaze over to the opposite bleachers where an older black woman was seated with a group of kids gathered around her.

Stanley grimaced and exclaimed, "Oh, really. Well, you need to keep your eye on her then."

Sam seemed surprised and asked, "How do you mean?"

Stanley explained emphatically, "Miss Esther lives right next to me with all of those foster kids. They're all trouble. I'm pretty sure one of them stole my air pump."

Sam replied dismissively, "Oh, really? I'll be sure to do that."

Finally, Sam realized that Stanley was not going to be engaged in any further conversation, so Sam patted Cooper on the head, glanced at Stanley who ignored him, and turned and walked back toward the tractor to complete his maintenance duties.

Eventually, Stanley stood up and walked away from the ball field with Cooper dutifully trotting along beside him.

Baseball had always been an important part of Stanley's life and a major source of camaraderie between Stanley and his son Eddy. Stanley enjoyed balancing his roles between being a proud father and a committed baseball coach for Eddy's team.

Since Eddy had been gone, Stanley couldn't even find the joy he had once experienced through baseball. He wondered if anything would ever be the same again.

Since Stanley had not been able to find it within himself to continue his career as a writer, he almost resented the distraction and the release that Lisa seemed to find in her job at the fitness club.

Lisa had always enjoyed working out and staying physically fit. It made her feel better in two ways: there was the energy and healthy feeling she got from being in shape, and then there was the reaction she got from others who noticed how attractive she was.

As she glanced around the spacious health club floor with all of the gleaming equipment, mirrors, and various people going through their routines, Lisa could lose herself and her pain in the mindless activity of doing her job and instructing her clients.

As usual, James Stafford—a physically fit, attractive guy in his 30s—seemed to need Lisa's advice and attention more than anyone else. Lisa was not oblivious to his attraction to her, and since she seemed invisible to Stanley, she welcomed the attention.

When she had thoroughly given James Stafford instruction and a demonstration of a particular piece of exercise equipment, and at the point he seemed more interested in flirting than exercising, she excused herself and headed for the Cycle Studio.

Lisa noticed one of her friends and clients, Deb, peddling one of the cycles. As Lisa approached, Deb pointed toward James Stafford and asked, "So, would that guy be considered a client...or a perk?"

Lisa shrugged, feigning ignorance, and said, "I'm sure I don't know what you mean."

Deb exclaimed, "Lord have mercy. That man never takes his eyes off of you."

Lisa replied knowingly, "It's not the eyes I have to worry about."

Deb replied conspiratorially, "Ooooooh, really?!"

Lisa interjected, "Stop. I'm married."

Deb nodded at James Stafford and asked, "Does he know that?" Deb explained, "It's hard to tell when you're not wearing a ring."

Lisa looked down at her hand, almost embarrassed, and tried to explain to Deb—and maybe to her own conscience, "You know I don't wear it when I'm working."

Deb blurted, "I'm just saying. Not that I blame you, I mean..."

Lisa interrupted her and motioned for Deb to be silent, uttering, "Shh."

At that very moment, James strutted into the room. He smiled, holding eye contact with Lisa, and walked past them and got onto an exercise bicycle a short two stations away from them.

Lisa politely nodded at him.

Deb emotionally commented under her breath, "Aye, aye, aye. When was the last time Stanley looked at you like that?"

Lisa scolded her. "Deb, leave him alone."

Lisa began to walk away, but Deb got off the bicycle and followed her. When Deb caught up, she shot Lisa a sidelong glance and said, "He doesn't appreciate you. That's all I'm saying."

Lisa stopped at the door and turned to Deb and said emotionally, "Deb, his son died! The issue is a little more complex than if he 'appreciates' me or not."

Deb shot back, "He was your son, too!"

"Which is why I have patience for what he's going through!" Lisa responded then turned and walked out the door, leaving Deb behind.

As Lisa walked out of the fitness club and headed home for the day, she was struck by the fact that she wasn't sure if she loved or even liked Stanley anymore, but she was at least willing to defend him and her memories of the life they had once had.

CHAPTER 4

That night, everything seemed calm and peaceful in the Walters' neighborhood. The orderly rows of houses were well-maintained, and the mature trees that had been there for decades gave the neighborhood a permanent and stable feel.

Inside the Walters' kitchen, everything seemed orderly, but there was a quiet tension bordering on distress.

Lisa took store-bought chicken potpies out of the oven and automatically set them on the table. Stanley walked in with a magazine and sat down at his place without saying a word. He opened his magazine and started to read as if he were alone in the room.

Lisa said in a matter-of-fact tone, "Deb is having a garage sale to raise money for the Tigers' baseball uniforms. I'm going to take some of my old clothes."

She paused for a moment and continued cautiously. "Maybe we could clean out the garage and donate some things."

Stanley was totally oblivious to Lisa and seemed to be engrossed in his magazine. He muttered, "Sure, whatever."

Lisa, sensing she was being ignored, proclaimed, "Oh, and I think that guy from the club is finally going to ask me out."

Stanley answered mindlessly, "Great."

Lisa sighed and said, "Stanley, you're not listening to me."

Stanley replied with venom, "I'm listening. You're just not saying anything important."

Lisa suppressed her frustration and tried to change the subject. "So, how did it go today? Did you make any progress on your book?"

Stanley looked up for a brief second, glared at Lisa, and then began eating his pot pie.

Lisa tried to connect again. "I'm sorry if I upset you. I was just trying to have a little conversation."

Stanley shot back, "So you nag me."

Lisa got upset, raising her voice. "I'm not trying to nag you. I just wish you would talk to me."

Stanley slammed his magazine on the table in frustration, stared at Lisa, and challenged, "OK, talk!"

Lisa just stared at him. She was deeply hurt, once again. It seemed to her as if this was a constant state they were living in.

Stanley broke the silence. "Come on, talk. You have my undivided attention. TALK!"

Lisa stared at him in disbelief. Finally she tried to speak softly. "I just wanted to know if you have made any progress on your book. That's all."

Stanley's anger grew, and he blurted, "Why don't you say what you're really thinking!"

Lisa implored, "Stanley, don't do this again."

Stanley wouldn't or couldn't let it go. "Come on, Lisa. Say it. Ask me what I was thinking. How I could ever let that happen."

Stanley was broken. Lisa slumped over the table and began to cry. Stanley turned and announced, "I gotta go."

Through her tears, Lisa watched Stanley walk out of the room and slam the door as he left the house. She wasn't sure what to do or if anything could even be done. Their lives were shattered in a million pieces, and there didn't seem to be any way to put it all back together. She wasn't sure she even wanted to try anymore.

Lisa finally cleaned up the meager dinner dishes and went to bed alone. She slept fitfully all night and was jarred awake, once again, by the ever-present alarm clock. She felt old and exhausted as she rolled over and, once again, confirmed that the other side of the bed had not been slept in.

Lisa went to her closet and began sorting through her clothes and laying certain items she selected on the bed. She thought, *At least I can get a head start on things for Deb's garage sale.* She knew it was for a good cause as the Little League team certainly needed new uniforms.

Meanwhile, Stanley was out in the garage surveying the mess that had not been touched in many months. Stanley walked back and forth in front of the stack of boxes without really getting anything done.

Lisa finished gathering the items for the garage sale from her closet and took an empty box, walked into Eddy's room, and set the box on his bed. She looked at the various pictures of Eddy on the dresser, and she smiled softly. She took a deep breath and set her resolve.

Lisa walked over to the dresser and opened the top drawer. All of Eddy's clothes were folded and lined up neatly, just as they had been two years ago. She surveyed everything for a few moments, and then she began gathering items until she came across a baseball jersey with the number 7 on the back. She picked it up and held it to her face, breathing in the fragrance. She smiled, remembering better days. She folded the jersey and placed it back in the drawer as she continued gathering other clothes and setting them in the box.

Lisa felt guilty and triumphant at the same time as she gathered more of Eddy's things for the garage sale. She thought to herself that Eddy would be willing to sell any of his things if he knew the funds would go to buy new baseball uniforms. Eddy would have lived in his baseball uniform if Lisa would have let him. He was convinced that once you made the baseball team and got a real uniform, you didn't really need any other clothes.

Lisa feared Stanley's reaction to her removing things from Eddy's room, but she believed that an angry reaction would be preferable to being ignored. Something had to change in their lives, and Lisa was confident that it couldn't get much worse.

CHAPTER 5

Lisa carried the box that contained the items to be donated for the garage sale to raise money for new Little League baseball uniforms. She had found a lot of unwanted clothing and household items for the sale, but as she walked out of the house onto the front porch carrying the box, she could only think of Eddy's things that she had removed from his room. The box wasn't very heavy to carry, but the emotional weight of anticipating Stanley's reaction to her getting rid of Eddy's things was unimaginable.

Lisa carried her box down the front steps and along the sidewalk to Deb's house where tables were already set up in the garage and on the driveway for the upcoming sale. Deb and her 10-year-old daughter Alexandra were already hard at work.

Alexandra, or Alex as she insisted on being called, was wearing a worn and tattered Tigers baseball uniform. Deb thought that Alex's uniform had to be good advertising for the sale because it was obvious that new baseball uniforms were badly needed.

As Lisa reached Deb's driveway, she could see that Deb had the baby on her hip as she was making preparations for the garage sale. Lisa sat down her box, greeted Deb and Alex, and kissed the baby.

Just as all of the items Lisa had brought had been displayed in an orderly manner on the various tables, Miss Esther and her kids approached from down the street.

Miss Esther, a dignified woman of undetermined age, had become a fixture in the neighborhood. She took in an ongoing stream of foster kids so it was hard to keep up with all of the young people who moved in and out of her house as if there were a revolving door.

As she walked up Deb's driveway, Esther was accompanied by Josh, the 10-year-old pitcher on the Tiger's baseball team. Her tattered uniform matched Alex's.

Rachel was a 7-year-old girl who had not spoken for several years. Rachel was carrying her worn rag doll that she was never without. Half the doll was burned, and Rachel had an angry burn scar on her arm.

Cody, was an 11-year-old boy who was cheerful and optimistic in spite of the fact that he had muscular dystrophy and was confined to a wheelchair.

The final member of Miss Esther's entourage on that day was Austin, a 15-year-old with a Jonas Brothers haircut. Austin always seemed to have his face in a video game, and he generally only grunted when spoken to.

Deb waved at the group and called, "Hi, Miss Esther. How are you?"

Miss Esther smiled warmly and replied, "Good, dear. Thank you for asking. I've got a box of items for your sale."

Deb looked at Esther's box and said, "Thank you. You didn't have to do that."

Josh and Alex, who were not only teammates but best friends, paired up and began digging through all of the items for sale on the tables. The other kids began walking among the tables to look at the various items being sold.

Rachel seemed drawn to one particular table that displayed a doll cradle with a blanket inside of it. She reached in and picked it up. Josh noticed and quickly moved over to Rachel.

She scolded, "Rachel, you need to put that back. It's not yours."

Rachel did not answer but just looked away.

Lisa, noticing the exchange between the two girls, approached.

Josh took the blanket away from Rachel and started to put it back into the cradle.

Lisa spoke to Rachel. "Hi, honey. Would you like this blanket for your doll?"

Rachel remained silent and just looked off into the distance.

Josh looked at Lisa and explained, "She won't talk to you. She doesn't talk to anyone."

Lisa seemed shocked by this. She looked on as Rachel walked away and sat on one of the porch steps.

As Josh and Alex continued to browse the items on the tables, Miss Esther approached Lisa.

Deb smelled the baby's diaper and called to Alex. "Alex, honey. Take your brother in and change his diaper."

Alex made a disgusted face and spoke in a whiny voice. "Ewww! Gross, Mom."

Deb assumed the motherly tone and commanded, "Alexandra, do as you're told."

Alex was resigned to the situation and took the baby. Alex held the baby at arm's length as she carried him into the house.

Miss Esther nodded toward Rachel who was sitting on the steps and explained quietly to Lisa. "She hasn't spoken in several years. The poor dear. She's been through a lot."

Lisa looked at the forlorn little girl and murmured, "Oh, I'm so sorry."

Miss Esther spoke with confidence. "Though I believe she will be better."

Miss Esther turned her gaze toward Josh and declared, "I thank the good Lord for Josh. I'd be lost without her."

Lisa and Miss Esther looked on as Josh sat by Rachel and fixed her hair with a bow.

Deb took a peek into Miss Esther's box. She called, "Wow! Look at all this great stuff!"

In Miss Esther's box were items from all over the world. There was a crane bell from India, a prayer candle from Mexico, and a hammock from Brazil.

Deb looked up at Miss Esther and asked, "Where did you get all of this?"

Miss Esther responded, "Oh, all over, I guess. Really don't have much use for it. With Josh on the ball team, I thought I could put it to good use."

As Alex returned with the baby freshly changed and handed him to Deb, Miss Esther opened her purse and lovingly took out an old oil lamp.

She spoke. "Oh, yes. And then there is this."

Alex seemed curious and said, "Look at that! What is it?"

Miss Esther paused and thought for a moment and then answered, "This is a very special oil lamp. I have the feeling it's time for it to find its new owner."

Alex seemed baffled and asked, "New owner?"

Miss Esther responded emphatically, "Yes, honey. This lamp will bring its owner the wisdom of the ages.

I've had it for quite some time now. I believe it's time for me to pass it along."

Deb and Lisa looked at one another as both were thinking that it was getting a little weird.

Lisa shrugged and said dismissively, "OK, great. Well, thanks for bringing all of this by."

Deb addressed Miss Esther in a formal tone. "On behalf of the Tigers New Uniform Committee, I thank you for your support."

Alex interjected, "Mom, it's time to go to practice. Can me an' Josh go to the field with Miss Esther?"

Deb corrected Alex's grammar. "Mean Josh? I don't think she is mean."

Alex rolled her eyes and had a disgusted look on her face as she said grudgingly, "Fine. May Josh and I go with Miss Esther to the field?"

Deb glanced toward Miss Esther who nodded her approval.

Deb looked back to Alex and said, "Go on."

Alex and Josh smiled at one another and exchanged high fives.

Miss Esther lovingly gathered up her makeshift family, and they all headed for the ball field in the park.

Lisa glanced from the oil lamp to Miss Esther and back again.

CHAPTER 6

Stanley sat alone at the desk in his home office, staring at the blank computer screen. The blinking cursor stared back at him as if to mock and ridicule his inability to write. Stanley knew that Lisa would be at the neighborhood garage sale most of the day, so he had fleetingly hoped that there might be a slight crack in the writer's block that had been plaguing him.

Cooper sat quietly in the corner and looked at Stanley as if he wanted to help.

Stanley placed his fingers on the keyboard with anticipation, but nothing would come. He turned away in frustration.

The light blinked on the answering machine signaling Stanley that more bad news was being piled on to their already desperate situation.

Eventually, he gave up, rose from the desk, and walked out of the office with Cooper following.

Stanley walked down the hall. He glanced into Eddy's room as he was passing and noticed instinctively that something was wrong. Stanley rushed into his son's bedroom and noticed that the dresser drawers were open. He moved quickly to the dresser and looked inside a drawer. Stanley felt as if he had been stabbed in the heart as he saw that Eddy's things had been disturbed and many items were missing.

It had been a long and hectic day at the garage sale. Deb and Lisa had rushed around frantically, assisting people who wanted to buy items to help the baseball team purchase new uniforms. By the end of the day, the tables that had been neat and orderly in the morning were now covered haphazardly with the remaining few items that had not sold.

Deb and Lisa began collecting the unsold inventory and packing the items in boxes to be delivered to Goodwill.

Deb turned to Lisa, sighed wearily, and said, "Thanks again for your help, hon."

Lisa nodded and said, "Glad to. To be honest, I would rather spend the day here instead of watching Stan stare at his computer screen."

Lisa was gathering the last few remaining items as she saw the old oil lamp at the end of the table. She picked it up and asked, "What should we do with this?"

Deb shrugged and said offhandedly, "I don't know. Take it with the rest of the stuff to Goodwill."

Lisa stared at the lamp she held in her hands and said, "I feel funny doing that. Maybe I should take it back to her."

Deb waved dismissively and replied, "I don't want it."

Lisa and Deb were interrupted when Alex stuck her head out of the front door and called, "Mom, I'm hungry."

Deb called back to her daughter. "Just a minute, babe. I'll be there in a sec."

Alex went back inside.

Deb blurted out, "You'd think the kid could make a sandwich or something. Kids. They'll drive you nuts if you let them."

Just then, Deb was struck by the insensitive words she had spoken to Lisa.

Deb said with anguish, "I'm sorry, hon."

Lisa tried to hide her pain and answered, "No, you're fine."

Lisa gathered all of her items and prepared to leave. Deb was upset with herself and gave Lisa a big hug.

As Lisa walked away, Deb called after her. "Call me later, OK?"

Lisa responded with more cheer than she felt. "OK, night."

As Lisa arrived back in her own driveway, she could see that the garage door was open but the mess seemed to have been untouched. She sighed, put down her box, and picked up Miss Esther's oil lamp. She held it before her for a moment as if making up her mind and then walked toward Miss Esther's house.

The last light from the sunset was fading away as Lisa stepped onto Miss Esther's porch and knocked. Austin came to the door.

Lisa smiled uncomfortably and asked, "Is Miss Esther here?"

Austin just grunted and walked away, and Lisa was left standing alone on the porch holding the battered old oil lamp. Finally, Miss Esther came to the door and saw Lisa standing there.

She said, "I'm sorry, child. How long have you been standing out here?"

Lisa shrugged and replied, "Oh, just a minute."

The silence drew out between them and became awkward. Finally, Miss Esther spoke up. "Can I help you with something?"

Lisa seemed to be lost in thought as she stood on the porch holding the lamp. Finally, she realized Miss Esther had spoken to her, and she blurted out, "Oh, yes, um, the lamp. It didn't sell."

Miss Esther smiled knowingly and said, "That doesn't surprise me."

Lisa had a questioning look on her face.

Miss Esther explained, "Well, it's not going to go to just anyone. It has to go to the right person. Looks to me like it might be you."

Lisa was perplexed and wasn't sure what she should do next. Her thoughts were interrupted by Esther saying, "Night, dear."

Before Lisa could say goodnight, Esther had closed the front door, and Lisa was left alone, standing on the porch holding the lamp. She shrugged and said to no one, "OK, then."

Lisa turned, walked down Esther's porch steps, and moved toward her own house. She was filled with a combination of hope and dread that she didn't fully understand, but somehow Lisa was convinced that—for better or worse—things were going to change.

CHAPTER 7

Stanley's anger and frustration built throughout the day. He just couldn't believe she had done it. Eddy's precious things were gone.

Stanley stood looking out the front door as Lisa approached the house in the growing darkness.

As Lisa entered the front door, Stanley was pacing back and forth in the living room like a caged tiger.

Stanley glared at her accusingly and asked, "So, where have you been all day?"

Lisa felt dread but smiled innocently and said, "I was at the garage sale. I told you."

Stanley threw down the gauntlet, declaring, "I was in Eddy's room today."

Lisa didn't know what to say, so she just looked at Stanley and waited.

His anger built as he questioned, "Just who do you think you are?" He paused, unable to control his anger, and continued. "What did you do with it?"

Lisa's mind was racing, but she couldn't find anything to say.

Stanley glared at her and blurted, "You didn't!"

Lisa tried to remain calm and explained, "I just thought we could put it to good use."

Stanley was furious. "How could you do that?!"

Lisa had heard enough. She finally reached the boiling point and threw Stanley's anger back at him. "Do what, Stanley? Get on with my life?"

Stanley was indignant and ordered, "Don't start with me!"

Lisa said imploringly, "It's been two years."

Stanley mocked her saying, "Two years. You make it seem like that is a long time."

Lisa sighed as if she felt the weight of the world and declared, "It *is* a long time."

Stanley continued the assault demanding, "How can you be so cold? He was your son, too."

Lisa matched his emotion as she said, "You don't think that I know that? You don't think that I miss him every moment of every day?"

"You sure don't act like it. You go on as if it never happened," Stanley countered.

Lisa collected her thoughts and tried to speak reasonably. "Stanley, listen to me. It's time to move on."

Stanley pointed his finger at her accusingly and announced, "You had no right. You're just throwing away his memory."

Lisa was tired of the fighting and everything it represented. She turned and walked away from Stanley. She crossed the room, sat on the couch, and placed the lamp on the coffee table in front of her.

Lisa couldn't look Stanley in the eye as she admitted, "Stanley, I can't do this anymore."

"Do what?" he shot back.

Lisa waved her arms, gesturing toward Stanley and everything in the room by way of explanation. "This! This constant arguing."

Stanley became defensive saying, "So now it's my fault. You blame me for all of this."

Lisa spoke before she thought. "Well, I wasn't the one watching him."

This hit Stanley like a hammer to the head as he spoke. "I knew it! You blame me. You have always blamed me."

Lisa tried to repair the damage her words had caused, saying, "No. I'm sorry. I didn't mean to say that."

Stanley rejected her apology stating, "Well, it's too late. You said it."

Lisa tried one more time saying, "Stanley, stop. I didn't mean it."

He couldn't hear her soothing words as his anger boiled over. He shouted, "You call yourself a mother.

Where were you? And now…now you just take what we have left of him, and you sell it to the highest bidder."

Lisa was totally broken.

Stanley continued. "Then you come home with this."

He picked up the lamp and asked, "What is this?!"

Before Lisa could answer, Stanley threw the lamp into the corner of the living room, hitting a clay pot that shattered into pieces. Without saying another word, Stanley stomped out of the front door, slamming it behind him. Lisa just stared at the front door in disbelief.

As Stanley rushed down the porch steps and rapidly walked away from the house, Miss Esther was standing at her front window watching as the figure of Stanley retreated into the distance. Miss Esther bowed her head sadly as if she knew what had happened. She lowered her shade and walked away from the window.

Lisa dropped onto the couch, put her head in her hands, and cried until she felt she had nothing left. Then she took a deep breath, got up, and walked to the corner where she began cleaning up the shattered pieces of the broken pot.

She noticed the lamp sitting there. She picked it up and looked at it as if she had never seen it before. She noticed that there was something written on the side of the lamp. She took a closer look but couldn't make out the words. Lisa took her shirt sleeve and wiped the lamp. She buffed it to a nice shine and then was able to read the inscription.

She read the words aloud. "Just believe."

She smirked to herself and said, "I wish I could."

Just then, the lamp began to hum as if there were a large bee inside of it. Lisa could feel the vibration as she held the lamp in her hands. It scared her, and she dropped the lamp to the floor. It landed upright on its base. Lisa backed away from the lamp as if it were going to attack her.

The lamp continued to hum, and the light bulb in the ceiling got brighter and brighter until it popped, showering glass shards onto the floor. Lisa screamed.

The room was thrown into total darkness except for the street light streaming in through the front window. She stood there for a moment and then reached over to a table lamp next to the sofa and turned it on.

The oil lamp was still on the floor, surrounded by the broken pieces of the pot.

Just then, Lisa was startled as the doorbell rang.

CHAPTER 8

Lisa stared at the front door. She couldn't imagine who would be ringing her door bell.

She called out, "Ah, um, just a minute."

She took a few deep breaths and slowly walked toward the door. She looked through the peephole, not knowing what to expect. Her gaze fell on a sight she would not have expected or even imagined.

Standing on Lisa's front porch, was an elderly, well-dressed, black man wearing a suit, a hat, and carrying a cane. He looked like he had just stepped out of a 1950s detective movie or had just walked offstage after performing a Vaudeville magic act.

Lisa blinked several times, not believing her eyes, but every time she looked, he was standing there as before, just smiling at the closed front door.

Lisa spoke tentatively through the door. "Can I help you?"

The figure on her front porch responded with confidence. "No, actually, I'm here to help you."

Lisa didn't know what to think about his response and tried to get rid of him saying, "I'm not sure what you are selling, but this really isn't a good time."

Lisa was startled by his response that came through the still-closed front door. "Lisa, listen to me. I'm not selling anything. I'm here because you asked for me."

Lisa was stunned and blurted out a question. "How did you know my name?"

She heard his logical response. "It's here on this plaque. Stanley and Lisa Walters."

Lisa felt embarrassed and muttered, "Oh, yeah."

The gentleman on the front porch addressed Lisa. "I'm sliding my card under the door. Read it."

Lisa looked down at the base of her front door, and slowly a business card slid onto the floor. She picked it up and read it. Printed on the card in elegant script were the words *Just Believe* with a name under it: *Charles Montgomery III.*

He repeated by way of explanation, "I'm here because you requested me."

"Requested you?" Lisa asked.

He responded in a matter-of-fact tone, "Yes. I believe the exact words were *I wish I could*...believe, that is."

Lisa just stared in disbelief from the door to the card in her hand and back again.

From the other side of Lisa's front door, her visitor beckoned, "Now, if you would be so kind as to open the door, I will explain everything."

Lisa took a deep breath and slowly opened her front door. There he stood, a splendid figure who seemed right where he should be, even though he appeared to be out of place and from the wrong time.

His ebony skin seemed to glow from within. His eyes appeared to be filled with the excitement of a child while containing an ancient understanding.

Lisa stepped back as her visitor politely took off his hat. Cooper walked into the living room and scampered toward Charles. Lisa was shocked as Cooper seemed to know this man and somehow was glad to see him.

The gentleman declared formally, "There, now. This is much more pleasant. Allow me to introduce myself properly. My name is Charles Montgomery the third."

Lisa stammered out a question. "What are you, some kind of genie?"

Charles Montgomery III let out a hearty laugh, shook his head, and explained, "Oh, my dear. No. I am real. Genies are fictitious. I am more of a messenger."

Lisa was becoming more confused by the minute. She inquired, "A messenger?"

Charles walked into the center of the room and asked, "May I sit?"

Lisa spoke automatically. "Um, sure. Please."

Charles walked to the corner of the room and sat in a chair. Lisa sat at the end of the couch with her back to the door and put Charles Montgomery III's business card on the coffee table in front of her.

Lisa was in a daze and wondered whether or not she was dreaming all of this.

Charles sneezed, and Cooper immediately took a tissue from the box on the coffee table, walked across the room, and presented it to Charles.

Charles smiled fondly as if they were old friends and said, "Thanks, Coop old boy."

Charles blew his nose and continued on as if nothing strange had happened. Lisa was dumbstruck and looked on in amazement.

Charles cleared his throat, looked directly at Lisa, and spoke. "Let me explain if I may. What would you say if I told you that you could have anything you want in your life?"

Lisa shook her head and responded, "I don't know. I guess I would say I didn't believe you."

Charles chuckled and then continued. "Excellent choice of words. Let's say for a moment that what I am saying is true. You can have anything you want. What is that one thing you would want that would make your life complete?"

Lisa thought for a moment, then answered, "Well, Mr. Montgomery..."

He interrupted. "Please call me Charles."

Lisa nodded and continued. "OK, um, Charles. I don't know. I guess just to be happy."

Charles spoke thoughtfully. "Hmm. Happy. What does 'to be happy' mean to you?"

Lisa responded automatically, "I guess it would be no more fighting. To have life be like it was before."

Charles clarified. "Before Eddy, you mean."

Lisa was stunned and exclaimed, "How do you…"

Charles smiled reassuringly and said, "I know a lot about you, Lisa, which is why I am here. Now listen to me closely. What I am about to tell you will change your life. You can have anything you want, including true happiness, and I am going to tell you the secret of how to get it."

Just then, Stanley returned, walked through the front door and looked at Lisa.

He asked, "What are you doing?"

Lisa turned toward Stanley and explained, "Talking to Charles."

She turned back toward the chair in the corner and pointed, but Charles was gone.

CHAPTER 9

Lisa stared in amazement at the empty chair. She thought it was more than enough to handle losing her son, her marriage, and everything that mattered without now somehow losing her mind.

Lisa blurted out, "Where did he go?"

Stanley was bewildered and asked, "Who?"

Lisa started to explain. "Charl…"

Then she realized how absurd it would sound.

Stanley was clearly getting irritated as he said, "What is going on with you?"

Lisa was flustered as she tried to recount the recent surreal events. "Stanley, I don't know how to explain this. I was picking up the mess, and I read the lamp. The light burned out, and he was at the door. He gave me a card."

Lisa quickly glanced down at the coffee table, but Charles Montgomery III's business card was gone, too.

Stanley stared at her and said, "So, you're telling me you rubbed the lamp, and a genie popped out."

Lisa nodded and explained, "Not a genie. He said he was a messenger."

Stanley just stared at his wife in total disbelief. After several moments, he was able to speak. "Listen, Lisa. I can't continue to pretend that everything is going to be OK. I mean who are we fooling? You don't love me, and I don't love you."

Lisa just stared at Stanley as he talked. Deep down in her heart, she was almost relieved.

Stanley continued. "I'm gonna find an apartment this week. You can have everything. I'm just done."

Stanley turned abruptly and walked down the hallway to Eddy's bedroom.

Lisa's mind was reeling. She was trying to get a grasp on recent events. First, Stanley had walked out on her, and she hadn't known whether or not he would ever return. Then this Charles Montgomery III person had showed up. She had felt disbelief and hope at the same time. And finally, just as Stanley comes back home again, Charles disappeared into thin air.

She didn't know what to believe.

Lisa sat alone in the living room but when she couldn't get any answers to the growing number of questions in her head, she gave up, walked down the hallway to the bedroom, and went to sleep by herself once again.

The next morning, the sun shone brightly and everything seemed normal throughout the neighborhood. But in the Walters' home, both Stanley and Lisa knew everything was far from normal.

When Lisa awoke, she glanced beside her in the bed to confirm the fact that she was still alone. As she slipped into her robe, she tried to determine whether the events of the previous night were real or somehow part of her dreams.

She walked down the hallway and looked into Eddy's room expecting to see Stanley sound asleep. But to her surprise, the bed had been slept in, but Stanley was gone.

Lisa continued down the hallway and entered the living room where the bizarre events of the night before had taken place. She opened the front door to get some fresh air, leaving the screen door closed. She surveyed the scene before her in the living room and tried to determine where she should start to clean up the mess and put everything back in order.

Lisa was standing on a chair, replacing the light bulb in the ceiling, when she heard footsteps on the front walk approaching her door. She glanced through the screen door and saw Miss Esther framed in the doorway, looking at Lisa holding the new light bulb. A broad smile broke out on Esther's face.

Lisa called, "Good morning, Esther. Come in."

Esther walked into the living room, noticing the broken pottery shards on the floor next to the oil lamp. She looked up to see the burn marks on the ceiling where the light bulb had exploded the night before.

Miss Esther chuckled and said, "Well, I can only assume you have met Charles."

Lisa sighed in relief and responded. "Oh, good."

Lisa climbed down from the chair and continued, "I thought I was going crazy."

Miss Esther laughed heartily and explained, "He has that affect on people."

Lisa asked, "Who is he? Where did he come from?"

Esther shrugged and said, "Hmm. How do you explain Charles? I think I will leave that up to him."

Lisa plopped onto the couch and began crying.

She said, "Stanley is leaving me."

Miss Esther moved over to the couch and spoke comfortingly. "Oh, you poor dear. Let's choose to believe that there is a greater purpose for all of this."

Lisa somehow felt better hearing the soothing words. She smiled up at Esther. Lisa dried her tears and hugged Esther warmly.

They had never been close before, even though they were neighbors, but somehow since the lamp and Charles had come into their lives, Esther's calming presence seemed to be a lifeline of hope. The two women laughed and talked comfortably as they cleaned up the living room and put everything back in its place.

When their work was done, Lisa surveyed the living room that looked like nothing out of the ordinary had ever happened there. Then she glanced at Esther who was smiling at her.

Somehow Lisa knew that things were going to be changing around the Walters' household. The pain was still ever-present, and hope seemed to be an elusive target that was hard to grasp.

She didn't know what the day would hold, but she was pleased to be moving away from all the yesterdays and everything they represented.

Esther looked at Lisa and winked, then she glanced down at the lamp and chuckled as she walked out the front door and back toward her house.

CHAPTER 10

Without thinking about where he was going or what he was doing, somehow Stanley ended up at the park sitting in an old set of bleachers in the outfield. Cooper was lying contentedly at Stanley's feet. Stanley was watching the kids practice on the field in front of him. In some way he didn't fully understand, when he watched them playing baseball, he could lose himself in the game and didn't have to think about anything else.

Sam was on a riding lawn mower when he spotted Stanley and Cooper. Sam pulled up and stopped in front of them and got off of the mower.

Sam called, "Well, hello again."

Stanley just nodded and didn't even glance away from the baseball diamond. Sam sat down on the bleachers just as if he had been invited to join Stanley and Cooper.

They sat in silence for a moment, and then Sam commented offhandedly, "You look like you have a lot on your mind."

Stanley muttered, "That's an understatement."

Just then, they both noticed the coach trying to help a player who was up to bat.

Stanley commented, "Look at that guy. He has no idea what he is doing."

Sam nodded and replied, "Bless his heart. He is doing the best he can. They could really use someone who knows what they are doing to help coach."

Stanley responded emphatically, "Me? Not interested. Those days are long gone."

They watched with interest and excitement as Josh wound up and whipped a ball over the plate. The batter swung awkwardly, missing the ball by at least a foot.

Stanley seemed excited as he stated, "Man, that girl has got an arm."

Sam prodded, "They could really use your help. From what I hear, you are quite the coach."

Stanley was getting annoyed and barked, "From what you hear? I'm not sure what you have heard, but I think you need to drop it."

Sam was persistent as he spoke. "Maybe you need them just as much as they need you."

Stanley refused to take the bait and blurted, "What makes you think you know what I need?"

Sam was undaunted as he responded. "I'm just saying…maybe this could help you with your loss."

Stanley spoke from his pain. "What do you know about my loss? Have you held your son in your lap… and…"

He was unable to finish his thought.

Sam feared he had gone too far and said, "I'm sorry, Stan. I just think that…"

Stanley got up to leave and spoke angrily. "Just mind your own business. You don't know me. You don't know what I need. Come on, Coop."

Stanley walked away, leaving Sam sitting on the bleachers. Cooper looked from Sam to Stanley, seeming to contemplate the inequities of life, then he resignedly trotted after Stanley.

Stanley's anger built and swelled as he walked back home. As he entered the living room, Lisa was folding clothes. Stanley noticed the mess had been cleaned up, and the lamp was sitting on the edge of the coffee table.

Cooper followed him into the room, then moved toward his pillow in the corner where he laid down to observe the couple.

Stanley simply blurted out, "Hey."

Lisa looked at him, knowing from experience that he had something to say.

Lisa calmly stated, "I don't want to fight."

Stanley let out a long, slow breath and agreed. "I don't either."

Lisa began. "I know you didn't believe me when I told you about Charles. I didn't really believe it myself, but Miss Esther came by today, and she told me he was for real."

Stanley was exasperated, and it was all he could do to hold his temper back. He took a deep breath and tried to speak calmly. "Lisa, please. There is no magic genie that is going to come out of a lamp and make everything all better."

Lisa pleaded, "But what if it is real? What if he can help us?"

Stanley's anger finally boiled over. He shouted, "You want to know what is real? I'll show you what's real!"

Stanley lunged toward the coffee table, picked up the lamp, and walked out the front door with great resolve. Stanley bounded down the front porch steps and hurried down the driveway. Lisa and Cooper hastily followed in his wake.

Lisa called out, "Stanley, what are you doing?"

Stanley ignored Lisa's question, rushed to the end of the driveway, and grasped the lid on one of the trash cans that had been placed at the curbside. In one motion, he removed the lid and forcefully threw the lamp into the trash can. He banged the lid back in place.

Lisa implored, "Stanley, stop!"

Stanley grabbed Lisa by the arms as if to wake her from a dream. He blurted, "There is no genie! There is no magic!"

Stanley turned and marched back to the house. Lisa and Cooper followed resignedly.

Stanley rushed up the steps, crossed the front porch, and forcefully threw open the front door. Stanley instantly stopped in his tracks and was dumbstruck by the sight before him.

As Lisa and Cooper reached the front door, they joined Stanley as he stared at the lamp that was sitting on the coffee table exactly where he had picked it up a few moments before.

Stanley blinked several times, looked at Lisa, and then back toward the coffee table where the lamp stood as a symbol of everything that couldn't be true. It was impossible to accept the fact that the lamp was sitting there, but there it was.

CHAPTER 11

There are certain sights, sounds, and events that cause us to question our understanding of reality. We tend to consider things to be within the realm of possibility because they have happened—or could have happened—before. Stanley and Lisa stared at the lamp sitting on the coffee table and were forced to question everything.

The living room was silent. Time stood still. Finally, Stanley turned to Lisa and uttered, "What the... How did you do that?"

Lisa shrugged and asked, "What are you talking about?"

By way of answer, Stanley just pointed to the lamp as they both continued staring at it in disbelief. Finally, Stanley reacted out of frustration and anger. He grabbed the lamp forcefully and rushed back out the door and toward the garage.

He flung open the garage door with one hand as he continued to hold the lamp tightly in the other. With conviction, he walked over to the workbench, banged the lamp down on it, and picked out a large hammer.

Lisa arrived at the garage and stood behind Stanley, calling, "Stanley, no! Stop!"

Stanley ignored Lisa and began violently beating the lamp with the hammer. He spoke to himself as he pounded the lamp with all of the anger, guilt, and frustration that had been building up in him for years.

Lisa began pacing behind him in disbelief, pleading, "Stanley, stop!"

Lisa finally gave up and walked out of the garage with Cooper following. She rushed into the back door of the house. Cooper paused on the driveway and looked back toward Stanley.

Stanley continued pounding mercilessly on the lamp. He spoke to it. "There. I'd like to see you escape that one."

Stanley was breathing hard from his exertion. He took what was left of the flattened and destroyed lamp and walked back toward the house with resolve. Cooper followed, adding the experience to the growing list of human behaviors he did not understand.

As Stanley entered the back door, he saw Lisa standing at the kitchen sink staring out the window.

Stanley walked over to where Lisa was standing. He continued to hold what was left of the lamp as they both stared out the window.

Stanley thrust the lamp in front of Lisa and stated emphatically, "Take a good look, Lisa. It's just a hunk of metal."

Lisa was on the edge of tears and said quietly, "You're just mean."

Stanley restated his belief. "There's nothing magical about it."

They both stood there in silence until they heard a noise behind them in the kitchen. As Stanley and Lisa both turned around in unison, they saw Charles calmly sitting at the kitchen table with a cup of coffee in his hand.

He spoke. "Are you sure there's nothing magical about it, Stanley?"

Stanley and Lisa looked at the lamp in Stanley's hand and were shocked to see that it had returned to its original form.

Stanley cried, "What the...?" and dropped it as if it were on fire.

Charles said, "Careful with that. It's an antique."

Lisa bent down and gently picked up the lamp. Stanley just stood, staring at Charles. Charles extended his leg and pushed a chair out from the table.

Charles looked up at Stanley and said, "Stanley, how about you take a seat, and we can have a talk."

Stanley complied with Charles's orders as he sank into the chair that had been offered. Lisa joined them and took a seat at the table.

Stanley couldn't find his voice but finally stammered, "What…? Who…? Who are you?"

Charles sat up straight, nodded formally, and spoke, "Charles Montgomery the third at your service."

Stanley asked, "Are you really a genie from that lamp?"

Charles was clearly irritated with Stanley's question. He responded, "Genie? Let me show you something."

Charles pointed at the microwave oven, and instantly the door turned into a high definition screen. Music that sounded like the theme from *I Dream of Jeannie* began to play, and a woman who looked like Barbara Eden in a genie outfit appeared on the screen. Then the screen changed to look like an old movie clip showing a big, bald genie with blue skin. Next, the screen revealed a scene from a cartoon with a genie and a magic lamp. And, finally, the screen shifted to a television commercial featuring Mr. Clean dressed as a genie.

Charles pointed to the images on the screen and stated, "Look here. Genie. Genie. Genie. Genie. Do I look like a genie?"

The screen went blank, and the microwave appeared normal once again.

Stanley and Lisa stared open-mouthed at Charles.

Stanley mumbled, "Sorry."

Charles sighed and spoke conciliatorily. "No, I'm sorry. It's just a bit of a sore spot for me. To answer your question, Stanley, I am a messenger. I am here to help you see beyond yourself and your current situation."

Stanley glanced toward Lisa and then looked back at Charles as he spoke. "I don't know what to say."

Charles explained, "You are correct, Stanley. There is no magic to this. You see, you can have anything you want in life if you are only willing to first believe. You and Lisa are in a tough spot...mainly because you have lost hope. Right now, you believe that there is no way out other than to give up."

Stanley and Lisa just stared at Charles as he continued. "Don't feel bad. This happens to a lot of people. Many people get their eyes off of what is true and embrace a lie. Then they begin to believe that lie. In time, this lie becomes their truth, and their whole life is built around it."

Stanley was trying to comprehend this. He voiced his question. "A lie?"

Charles nodded solemnly and answered, "Yes. For you, it's the lie that your life ended the day your son died. You cannot forgive yourself for this terrible event, and so you punish yourself and those around you. The truth, Stanley, is your life can and should go on. You must let go of the pain, and live your life to its fullest."

Stanley was disturbed, and his anger flared as he said, "That's easy for you to say."

Charles shrugged and admitted, "Yes, I guess it is. Because I believe that life should be lived even when a tragic event has occurred."

Charles paused a moment to let his words sink in, and then he continued. "My message is this—that you can have anything you want in life, even happiness and forgiveness, if you are willing to just believe."

Stanley just stared at Charles, not knowing what to say, do, or think.

CHAPTER 12

The Walters' kitchen, which had been a familiar and comfortable place to Stanley and Lisa, now seemed strange, unusual, and hard to understand. The appearance of Charles had left the couple reeling.

Stanley confronted Charles saying, "I think it would have been better if you were a genie. You could grant me my three wishes, and I could wish my way out of this."

Charles laughed heartily and said, "Well now, that's an interesting idea. Hmm. Three wishes. I don't normally do that, but if that helps you, then three wishes it is."

Stanley sounded skeptical as he said, "Let me get this straight. You are going to give me three wishes? I can have anything I want?"

Charles nodded and explained, "Yes, but there will have to be some rules."

As Stanley and Lisa looked on, Charles took a sip of his coffee and opened a book that suddenly appeared on the table in front of him. Then a pair of reading glasses suddenly appeared in his hand, and he put them on.

Charles looked at the couple and said sheepishly, "You'll have to forgive me. I've never been real good with all the legal parts."

Charles opened the book then reached into his vest pocket and took out an ornate writing pen. He began making notes in the book.

Charles scanned a page, glanced at another, then spoke. "So, let's set some guidelines."

He smiled at the couple, cleared his throat, then continued to speak formally as he read from the book. "When said wishes are granted, Wisher...that's you..."

He glanced up at the couple and pointed at them, then continued. "cannot present a wish that will: One. Interfere with another person's free will."

He paused and smiled at the couple, then said, "Two. Bring someone back to life."

Charles appeared a bit uncomfortable as he said, "Ah, yes, that is vital in this case, isn't it?"

He looked at the couple solemnly, then glanced back at the book as he continued. "And Three. This one is important. Said wish cannot be something Wisher has the power to acquire on his or her own."

He stopped and looked up at the couple and announced, "Yes, I like that one. So, there you have it. Oh, yes. And let's put a time limit on it. Say, 30 days."

Charles closed the book and slipped it into his vest pocket. Stanley and Lisa were speechless.

Stanley wasn't sure he believed any of this, but he asked, "It can be anything?"

Charles held up his finger to emphasize his point. "Within the rules."

Stanley and Lisa nodded in unison.

Charles leaned forward and said in a conspiratorial tone, "On a personal note, it is my belief that this experience will bring your heartbeat back."

"My heartbeat?" Stanley asked dubiously.

Charles nodded excitedly and exclaimed, "Yes. Listen closely."

The room fell silent as they all listened.

Charles asked, "Do you hear that?"

Stanley and Lisa had blank expressions as they both shook their heads no.

Charles was confident as he said, "Listen closer."

Stanley and Lisa were shocked as they began to hear the sound of a soft, rapid heartbeat.

Charles asked, "Do you hear how fast it is?"

Stanley and Lisa nodded vigorously.

Charles explained, "That's because it is a woman's heartbeat. Always a little faster than a man's. Not many people know that."

Stanley looked toward Lisa as they both realized the incredible fact that they were hearing her heart beating.

Charles turned to Stanley and asked, "Stanley, I bet you haven't heard your heartbeat in a while, have you?"

Stanley was taken aback by the question and could only manage to shake his head no.

Charles spoke directly to Stanley. "I want you to hear your heartbeat again. You will hear it when your life is in rhythm, and there is no doubt that you're doing what you were made to do. That's your heartbeat. That's when you're truly alive and not just existing. I want you to get your heartbeat back. You can if you are willing to believe you can."

Charles nodded and gave the couple a big smile.

He announced, "So, I guess I'll see you in 30 days. And remember, all things are possible if you just believe they are."

Stanley and Lisa continued to stare at Charles as he stood up.

Charles muttered to himself, "Yes, this part is always awkward, isn't it?"

He pointed at something behind Stanley and Lisa, and called, "Hey! What's that?"

Stanley and Lisa quickly whirled around to see what he was pointing at, but everything seemed to be in its place and appeared normal. When Stanley and Lisa turned back toward Charles, he had disappeared.

The couple sat silently and stared at one another. They got up from the table and looked around the room as if Charles might have left some clue behind that would confirm he had truly been there, and all of this was really happening.

Stanley rounded the table and stared closely at the chair where Charles had been sitting. Lisa opened and closed the microwave door several times, but everything seemed frustratingly normal.

Stanley and Lisa had been drifting apart for so long they had lost any point of contact or connection in their lives. Somehow they knew that this bizarre and mysterious experience they had witnessed together in their own kitchen could be the beginning of a new life for them. Whether or not Charles was real or wishes could come true, Stanley and Lisa felt a glimmer of hope.

Eventually, the couple drifted out of the kitchen, and Lisa got ready for bed. As she lay down, she hoped Stanley would join her, but he didn't appear.

Stanley sat at the computer in his home office as he had done for days on end, staring at the blank computer screen, but somehow this night felt different. He placed his fingers on the keyboard and smiled. The old familiar creative juices seemed to be flowing.

CHAPTER 13

The next morning, Lisa woke up well-rested a few minutes before the alarm clock blared. She glanced beside her and confirmed that Stanley was not on his side of the bed, but somehow Lisa felt hope instead of the despair that generally greeted her each morning.

She didn't know what to think about the events of the previous day, but she just kept telling herself to take it one step at a time and see where this new path led.

Lisa got ready for work and headed to the kitchen for a quick cup of coffee. The lamp was sitting in the middle of the table. She stared at it for a moment, repeating the message inscribed on the side of the lamp.

"Just believe. Just believe..."

Lisa took a deep breath and gathered her things to leave for the day. Then she hurried down the hallway to the office to grab her car keys.

As Lisa stepped into the office, something was different. The atmosphere seemed charged, and there was an energy that hadn't been there before—or at least for several years.

Lisa reached for her keys on the desk and as she did, she noticed the computer screen.

Lisa was so used to seeing the screen blank that when she saw the typed words, she did a double take. The screen read: *Just Believe—If you could have anything you wanted, what would it be?*

Lisa smiled and nodded enthusiastically. Somehow, those few words made a huge difference in her mind and spirit.

Lisa grabbed her keys and hurried out of the office with a spring in her step.

Stanley, having experienced his first literary inspiration in more than two years, was daring to be hopeful. He hadn't written much, but he had the spark of an idea. In the old days when he was a prolific writer, he knew such a spark could burst into a raging fire.

Stanley decided to do some work on the mess in the garage. He climbed over the debris and made his way to the back of the garage to survey the task at hand. He walked back to the front of the garage and looked out the large door to see Miss Esther's kids playing in the yard.

Stanley shook his head, turned, and looked at the complete mess that confronted him. He spoke to himself with resolve.

"Well, here we go."

Stanley walked over to his tool bench at the side of the garage and began by organizing some of the tools that were scattered everywhere.

Stanley could hear Miss Esther's kids playing as he worked. Josh was throwing a baseball back and forth with Austin and Cody while Rachel sat on the porch steps playing with her rag doll.

Josh taunted, "Come on, Austin. Throw the ball with your boy arm this time."

Josh threw the ball to Cody who laughed and threw the ball to Austin.

Cody continued the banter. "Yeah, Austin. Use your boy arm."

Austin turned to Josh and called, "Shut up! I can throw a lot harder than you."

Austin wound up and threw the ball with all his might. It sailed over Josh's head and into the Walters' garage where it hit Stanley in the rear end. Cooper was lying on the floor and watched the ball bounce off of Stanley and hit a can of nails that scattered all over the garage floor.

Stanley cried, "Ow!" as he turned and looked in the direction from where the ball had been thrown. Stanley looked around on the floor and found the ball.

He hurried over, picked it up, and angrily headed for the garage door.

The kids were wide-eyed and giggling, but when Stanley stepped out of the garage holding the baseball, they scattered. Austin bolted for the house and ran inside while Cody raced away in the opposite direction.

Stanley yelled after them. "Hey, you brats. Learn how to throw."

Josh didn't run. She was nervous, but she held her ground.

Stanley muttered to himself, "Stupid kids."

Stanley threw the ball at Josh much harder than he should have, but with her quick reflexes, she deftly caught it.

Josh called to Stanley defiantly. "I know how to throw."

Stanley responded, "No, you don't."

Stanley walked back into the garage. Josh was offended and followed him as Rachel got up and followed Josh.

Stanley began picking up the nails that were scattered on the garage floor.

Josh walked in and said, "My coach says I have a great arm!"

Stanley spat back, "Well, then your coach is an idiot."

Josh would not be intimidated. She equaled Stanley's venom as she said, "Yeah? Well, whadda you know?"

Stanley shrugged and responded matter-of-factly, "Apparently more than your coach."

Josh couldn't let it go and refused to let Stanley win. She blurted, "Yeah, well at least I'm not a pervert or a crazy guy who talks to his dog."

Stanley stopped picking up the scattered nails on the floor, stood to his full height, and turned to stare at Josh in confusion.

She had a smirk on her face as she felt her comment had gotten to him.

Stanley appeared disoriented and asked, "What is that supposed to mean?"

Josh explained, "I've seen you watching our practices and talking to your dog."

Stanley didn't know how to respond to that. The garage fell silent.

Rachel was petting Cooper as if they were long-time friends.

Josh broke the silence with a question. "What are you doing watching us play all the time?"

This made Stanley mad. He blurted out, "None of your business, kid. Go away."

Stanley glanced at Rachel and Cooper and called, "Cooper, come here now!"

Stanley picked up the can of nails and walked back to his bench. Cooper moved over beside Stanley, and Josh walked away in a huff.

Josh called over her shoulder, "Come on, Rachel."

Rachel stood up and looked toward Stanley. Then she bent down and picked up a nail from the garage floor he had overlooked. She walked over and set it on the workbench then turned to walk away.

Stanley, for the first time, realized how harsh he had been with the kids and probably with everyone for the past couple of years. He thought that the first step toward solving the problems he faced was to admit that there actually were problems, and they belonged to him.

CHAPTER 14

Stanley stood in his messy garage watching Josh and Rachel walk away. He knew the anger and frustration he felt was not because of the girls. The unresolved issues in his life resembled his garage. There had been a lot of junk packed away for a long time.

Stanley called toward Josh's retreating back. "You sling it too much."

Josh turned and replied, "Excuse me?"

"Your arm," Stanley explained. "You have strength but not form."

Josh answered him defiantly, "I throw better than everybody else."

Stanley nodded in agreement with her and said, "But not as well as you could. Go over there, and throw me the ball."

Stanley pointed to the center of the driveway. Josh shrugged, willing to comply, but she was wary of Stanley and his temper.

Cooper snuck past Stanley and joined Rachel beside the driveway. Rachel began to pet Cooper as she watched the exchange between Josh and Stanley.

Josh threw the ball to Stanley.

He had almost forgotten his coaching technique and how much he loved working with kids. It came back to him quickly as he instructed Josh. "You see. Right there. You throw from your side."

Josh shook her head and disagreed. "No, I don't."

"Yes, you do," Stanley insisted. "It's…well, you throw like a girl. Just a bit."

Josh definitely didn't like Stanley's comments.

He demonstrated the throwing motion as he explained, "Gotta bring your arm back more, then up, over, and through."

Stanley threw the ball to Josh. She caught it and stood thinking for a moment as she ran through the new throwing motion in her head. Then she wound up and fired the ball to Stanley.

Stanley caught it and offered some constructive criticism. "Not bad. You're still using too much of your arm, though."

Josh seemed bewildered and asked, "What else would I use?"

Stanley explained, "You need to use more of your body or you'll just wear out your arm."

Josh stared at Stanley with a confused expression.

He demonstrated the throwing motion as he instructed, "Look here. If you shift your weight to your left leg a little sooner, you'll get more power in your throw."

Stanley used the technique he described as he threw the ball back to Josh. She caught it and really concentrated on her throwing motion as she wound up and hurled the ball at Stanley.

He reached out to catch it, but Josh had thrown it so hard it stung his hands.

Stanley cried, "Ow! Dang it!"

Stanley dropped the ball like a hot potato, and Josh smiled with satisfaction.

She called out playfully, "Don't you have a glove, mister?"

The thought of a baseball glove made Stanley think of Eddy which forced Stanley's lighthearted, good mood to shut down immediately. His demeanor and countenance shifted as he shook his head and replied sadly, "No. No, I don't. Not anymore."

Without any further explanation, Stanley just turned on his heel and walked back to the garage. He snapped his finger, and Cooper followed him. Josh stood alone in the middle of the driveway, hurt and confused.

Stanley resumed his efforts to clean up the mess in the garage. Cooper sat just inside the garage door looking at Rachel. Josh held the baseball and practiced her new throwing motion.

Stanley picked up a box to move it, but the bottom immediately fell out of the box, noisily dumping the contents onto the garage floor.

Josh and Rachel instantly ran to the garage to see what had happened, arriving just in time to catch Stanley venting his frustration loudly.

"Uuuggghhh!!"

Stanley looked up in exasperation and noticed the girls standing at the entrance to the garage, staring at him. Cooper had positioned himself alongside Rachel.

Josh asked, "Are you OK?"

Stanley just stared at the girls in frustration and sighed. Finally, without speaking, he began picking up the mess on the garage floor and putting the spilled items back into the box.

Josh was uncomfortable and wanted to reach out to Stanley, but she didn't know what to say. Finally, she began speaking about the only topic they seemed to have in common.

"So, where did you learn so much about baseball?"

Stanley was still picking things up off the floor and was caught off guard by her question. He asked, "What?"

"I mean," Josh inquired, "did you play when you were a kid or..."

Stanley confronted her with anger and impatience as he spoke. "Listen, kid. I don't have time for all your questions, so unless you want to pitch in and help, then just leave me alone, OK?"

Josh didn't know what to say. She was intimated and a little scared, so she just stood in silence.

Stanley nodded and continued. "Yeah, that's what I thought."

He resumed picking up spilled items and replacing them in the box. Josh didn't know what to say, but she defiantly joined Stanley in picking up the spilled contents.

Just then, Miss Esther stepped into the garage and asked, "Josh, what are you doing?"

Josh glanced up and explained in a matter of fact tone, "I'm helping Mr. Walters straighten up his garage."

Stanley turned around and gave Josh a curious look. Josh stared back at him without blinking.

Miss Esther looked toward Stanley and asked, "Is that true, Mr. Walters?"

Stanley was caught off guard but said, "Yeah, I guess it is."

Miss Esther smiled and said, "OK, then. Don't stay too long. You've got practice this afternoon."

Josh nodded and replied, "OK."

Miss Esther surveyed the scene in the garage another moment, got a knowing smile on her face, then turned and walked back toward her house.

Stanley turned to Josh and said, "Well, since it looks like I'm stuck with you, help me put the rest of this stuff back in this box."

Stanley and Josh made an awkward, mismatched pair, but somehow they instinctively knew that each might hold the key that could unlock the solution to the other's problem so that healing might finally begin.

CHAPTER 15

S tanley and Josh continued their efforts to clean up
the garage. They worked in tandem, and it seemed as
if the ice between them was melting, and somehow they
might be kindred spirits.

Stanley looked over at Rachel and asked Josh, "So,
what's her story?"

Josh looked up from her work and asked, "Whose
story?" She followed Stanley's gaze as he continued
looking at Rachel. Josh confirmed, "Who? Rachel?"

Stanley nodded and observed, "She doesn't talk
much."

Josh chimed in. "She doesn't talk ever. Not since the
accident."

Rachel played with Cooper as Stanley and Josh
continued their work.

Stanley was struck by the fact that he thought he might actually be forming a bond with these dysfunctional kids. He lamented the reality that he could at least carry on a conversation with them while he couldn't seem to open up any line of civil communication with Lisa. He wasn't sure if he still loved her, or even liked her, but unless they could find a way to talk, he knew they had nowhere to go.

Lisa silently shared Stanley's frustration at their inability to communicate. She remembered earlier and better times when they could talk for hours without running out of things to say or simply sit together in a satisfying, comfortable silence.

The rock of their relationship that had seemed so steady and indestructible had been instantly shattered in one fateful, tragic moment.

These thoughts were racing through Lisa's mind as she was in a private Pilates session with her friend and confidant, Deb. Lisa reveled in the fact that she could lose her pain and anguish, if only for a little while, in the physical exertion of exercise.

Deb broke Lisa's stream of thought as she asked, "So, can you borrow me 20 bucks?"

Lisa looked up and tried to hold back the smile that was forming on her lips. Deb always had a cute way of using borrow and lend interchangeably. She shook her head emphatically, replying, "No."

Deb was excited and implored, "I promise I'll pay you back tomorrow."

Lisa feigned a stern expression and solemnly stated, "I will not take part in your addiction."

Deb wasn't ready to give up. She continued. "Come on. This is a sure thing. I've got a sucker on the stair stepper who is willing to bet against OU." Deb stated without a shred of doubt in her mind, "The Oklahoma Sooners simply can't lose."

Lisa resumed her role as the Pilates trainer and implored, saying, "Come on. Concentrate on this."

Deb shook her head mockingly and said, "You're no fun."

Lisa ignored her and got Deb into another position.

Lisa's thoughts had never been far from Charles and his strange appearance in their lives. On one hand, she tried to dismiss it knowing that it couldn't be true, but on the other hand, it seemed and felt real, and Charles's three wishes challenged Lisa in ways that were strange but exciting to her.

Without thinking, Lisa turned to Deb and spoke. "Let me ask you a question. This might seem a bit strange, but go with me on it."

Deb shrugged and offered a blank expression, muttering, "OK."

Lisa wasn't sure where to start, so she just dove in, asking, "If you could have anything you wanted, what would you wish for? Oh, and it has to be something that you cannot get on your own."

Deb spoke as she thought. "Wish for anything I want that I can't get on my own. Hmm. That's easy. Money."

Lisa shook her head and declared, "You can get money on your own."

Deb chuckled and explained, "Not this kind of money. I'm talking crazy money. The kind that a rich uncle leaves you."

Lisa looked into the distance and pondered for a moment, then responded, "Yeah, I guess that works."

"Of course it does," Deb prodded. "And, unlike you, I would share it with my best friend."

Lisa smirked, looked at her friend, and said, "The answer is still no."

Lisa thought about the three wishes and the possibility of money being one of the things she might wish for. Money had certainly been a struggle in their lives, particularly in the early years of their marriage. Then, just when things were getting a little more comfortable financially, the tragedy with Eddy hit them, Stanley's career went into a tailspin, and money seemed to represent a constant crisis in the Walters' household.

Lisa wanted to talk to Stanley about money and the three wishes, but she wasn't sure how to talk to him or if he would even entertain the possibility. Lisa wasn't sure if the occasional angry exchange with Stanley was better or worse than the constant silence between them.

Lisa instinctively knew that, while communicating with Stanley could be hurtful to their relationship, silence would be fatal.

The process of cleaning the garage engaged Stanley in a way he had not experienced for a long time. The physical exertion left his mind free to wander, and it was never far from Charles, the three wishes, and Lisa.

As he continued cleaning up his workbench, he thought about Lisa and wondered what she was thinking and whether she had been considering the three wishes. There was a time when Stanley had felt like he knew what Lisa was feeling and thinking without talking to her. Now, even when they talked, they seemed like strangers.

Josh was picking up newspapers off of the garage floor and tying them together with string into bundles.

Stanley walked over to check on her progress, saying, "When you're done with that, we can haul them to the end of the driveway."

Josh spoke between deep breaths. "I haven't worked this hard since I stayed with the farmer."

Stanley was confused and asked, "How long have you been in foster care?"

Josh explained, "About three years. This is my fourth home."

Stanley was shocked. He exclaimed, "Really? Four foster homes in three years?"

"Yeah," Josh said sheepishly. "They tell me I have some anger issues."

Stanley replied, "Really?" as he considered Josh's anger and his own.

He realized that Josh's anger had caused her to have to move from home to home while his own anger was destroying the love and harmony in the home he had. Stanley looked at Josh thoughtfully and realized they were a lot alike.

CHAPTER 16

S tanley surveyed the garage and the progress he and Josh were making in their cleanup project. It appeared to Stanley that, in spite of their hours of hard work, somehow in the midst of the project the garage looked worse than it had when they had started. Maybe all progress begins with removing that which currently exists so that it leaves room for the things that might be possible.

Stanley wanted to avoid his own anger issues because it was easier to focus on Josh's.

He echoed her earlier admission. "So you have anger issues?"

Josh nodded thoughtfully and revealed, "I'm not looking for fights, but it's just not right for someone big to hurt someone small. Especially moms or kids. People who do that should be punished for what they do."

Stanley had a knowing expression on his face as he steadily gazed at Josh.

She continued. "I promised Miss Esther that I wouldn't fight anymore. She wants me to stay with her until DHS finds me a family."

Stanley asked, "Do you like living with Miss Esther?"

Josh nodded excitedly and said, "Yeah, she's great. But the real reason I am here is to take care of Rachel."

Stanley nodded and muttered thoughtfully, "I see."

Josh continued. "She doesn't have to talk to me. I know exactly what she is saying."

Stanley didn't know how to respond, so he didn't say anything.

Josh broke the uncomfortable silence and changed the subject, asking, "So, what else do you do besides take forever to clean your garage?"

Stanley was taken off guard and stammered, "Oh, um, well. Actually I'm a writer. I write books."

"Wow!" Josh exclaimed with childlike enthusiasm. "You must be rich."

Stanley thought how far from the truth that was and muttered, "Heh, not exactly."

Josh continued excitedly. "I wish I had a lot of money."

The comment impacted Stanley. He stopped tying bundles of newspapers and stood up straight.

He asked, "What did you just say?"

Josh looked at Stanley as he stared at her with a bewildered expression on his face.

She spoke uncomfortably. "I just said that I wish I had a lot of money."

Stanley felt he was on to something here and prodded, "And what would you do with it if your wish came true?"

Josh replied automatically, "Oh, I could do all kinds of things. Like buy Miss Esther a much bigger house, or new uniforms for my team. Or, I dunno, maybe finally get a family that would adopt me and Rachel. If I had money, someone would adopt us."

Stanley's immediate thoughts were of Eddy and the tragic loss in his own family.

He stated, "Yeah, well, some things even money can't fix."

Josh was uncomfortable as she sensed the major shift in Stanley's mood.

She said, "Well, I think I better be going. Come on, Rachel."

As Josh and Rachel began to walk away, Cooper followed them. Stanley snapped out of the mood created by memories of Eddy, and he went after the girls.

Stanley caught up with the girls just as they were approaching Miss Esther's porch.

He called, "Wait! Josh."

Josh and Rachel both stopped and turned around. Stanley reached into his pocket and took out a five dollar bill. Stanley handed the five dollar bill to Josh.

"Here," he said. "For your work."

Josh squinted at Stanley and seemed suspicious. She wouldn't take the money from him.

"You don't need to pay me," she announced.

Stanley replied, "Well, who said it was for you?"

Josh seemed perplexed.

Stanley continued. "It's to help your team. For the uniforms."

Josh smiled faintly and took the money.

She mumbled, "Thanks, but we're going to need a lot more than this.

Stanley responded, "Well, that garage ain't gonna clean itself."

Josh's smile widened a bit more, and she said, "Thanks for everything."

Stanley seemed perplexed and questioned, "Excuse me?"

"For the throwing lesson," Josh explained. "I think it will help."

Stanley shrugged and said, "Yeah, well, it was nothing."

Josh nodded, turned to Rachel, and said, "Come on, Rachel. Let's get inside."

Josh and Rachel headed for Miss Esther's front door. Cooper followed them.

Stanley called to him, "Stay here, Coop."

Cooper stopped, turned, and looked at Stanley. Then he looked back at the girls. Everyone was frozen in place for a moment. Then Stanley turned and walked back toward his garage.

Cooper gave the girls one last look. Then he turned and followed Stanley back home.

Stanley couldn't get Charles's wishes and Josh's ideas out of his mind. After working a little more in the garage, he retreated to his home office where he confronted the computer and actually formulated some of his thoughts into writing.

When Lisa got home that evening, she heard the joyous sound of the keyboard clicking down the hallway. She slipped silently to the door of the office and peered in. Stanley didn't notice her, but she could see some of the words he had typed on the screen. It read: MONEY. *What would I do if I could have all the money I ever wanted?*

As Stanley continued to type, Lisa moved silently down the hallway to their bedroom. As she got ready to go to bed and eventually drifted off to sleep, Lisa could hear typing continuing from the office down the hallway.

The sound and the anticipation put her in mind of earlier and better times in their lives. She remembered when all they had were some random thoughts Stanley would type into the computer, but somehow it had all worked out. She had never realized how fortunate they had been back then.

Ideas, hopes, and dreams were all they had, but that was all they had needed.

Chapter 17

Stanley typed away at the computer, working late into the night. He wasn't sure that what he was writing was any good, but he was afraid to stop. Stanley feared that if he shut off the flow of inspiration, he might not be able to find it and get it back again.

Eventually, his thoughts about wishes and money seemed to be complete. He didn't have all the answers, but he had at least formulated the questions.

He drifted off to sleep that night alone in Eddy's room, but he had the satisfaction of having done some work on a writing project. He wasn't sure if it would become a book or just remain random thoughts about Charles and the three wishes, but something was always better than nothing.

Once again, it was a bright and sunny day filled with joy and anticipation. Stanley was putting a helmet on

Eddy as the young boy proudly sat atop his bicycle that, for the first time in his short life, didn't have training wheels.

Stanley looked on proudly as he held the training wheels that he had just removed in his hand.

Eddy had an expression of great concentration as he started the bike rolling down the driveway.

Stanley's expression of excitement quickly shifted to one of great concern.

Stanley called out, "Slow down, Eddy. Watch where you're going."

Stanley started to run down the driveway. His heart was filled with fear and dread.

Stanley yelled frantically, "Eddy! Stop!"

Stanley was startled awake and realized he had, once again, relived the worst moment of his life. He was covered with sweat as he looked around the room to orient himself. He had woken up, once again, from the hideous nightmare in his son's room, surrounded with all of the memories.

The clock read 5:23 A.M.. Stanley was exhausted as he rolled out of bed. He had hoped that the inspiration of writing the night before might have vanquished the recurring dreams of that fateful day with Eddy.

Stanley put on the clothes he had worn the day before and walked down the hallway and out of the house.

Lisa woke up alone in the master bedroom. She thought she had heard something, but she couldn't be sure.

Lisa got out of bed and faced the new day with more hope and optimism than she had felt in a long time. The thought of Stanley writing again lifted her spirits.

After going through her morning routine of showering and dressing, Lisa went to the kitchen for her customary and necessary cup of coffee. As she entered the kitchen, she saw Cooper lying near the back door. His tail thumped a greeting on the floor.

Lisa downed her coffee quickly, and as she was putting the cup in the sink, she glanced out the window and saw Stanley walking out of the garage and heading down the driveway carrying tied bundles of old newspapers.

Lisa spoke to herself. "Well, I'll be."

Cooper responded with more of his wagging tail thumping the floor.

Lisa turned to him and said, "Go help Daddy, Coop, old boy."

Cooper stood up on cue, moved to the back door where a ball was tied to a string connected to the door knob. Cooper grasped the ball in his mouth and backed up which opened the door. He rushed out the door and down the steps toward Stanley.

Lisa watched Stanley and Cooper playing for a few moments. Then she gathered her things to get ready for work. As she went into the home office to get her car keys, Lisa stared at the back of the computer monitor. She listened to the silent house for a moment and then glanced around to make sure no one was watching. As she rounded the desk under the guise of reaching for her car keys, she sort of, accidentally, and kind-of-on-purpose hit the computer mouse so the image of a beach scene screensaver was replaced with the lines that Stanley had written the night before.

Lisa uttered a false and insincere, "Oops."

She smiled at the words MONEY, WISHES, and paragraphs of writing below. She was excited about the prospect of Stanley getting back to work, but all of a sudden she was overcome by the feeling that she wasn't alone.

Lisa glanced toward the office door and saw Cooper standing there, staring at her.

She stared back at him for a moment, then asked impatiently, "What?"

She knew she was busted as Cooper continued to stare at her with his penetrating eyes. She picked up her car keys and began to leave.

She glanced down at Cooper and said, "You keep your mouth shut."

She bent down, kissed Cooper on the top of his head, and rushed off to work.

Lisa could never explain to anyone how much those few words on the computer screen meant to her. For months on end, there had been nothing but a blank computer screen in their home office which signaled hopelessness and despair. Now, the sight of words on the screen shouted out the possibility of something **better** ahead.

Lisa was struck by the fact that, in the midst **of grief** and depression, it took so little to bring hope back **into** the picture. She wasn't convinced that everything **would** be all right or even get back to the way it had been **before**. But for the first time in a long time, Lisa thought **they** might survive.

CHAPTER 18

Stanley felt good to be busy doing something even if it was as mundane as making progress cleaning out his garage. It seemed to be a matter of two steps forward and one step back.

He was excited that he had been able to write the previous night for the first time in a long time, but the reoccurring nightmare involving Eddy and the tragedy was still there.

Then there was Charles and the bizarre thought of getting three wishes from a guy who apparently came from a magic lamp.

Stanley sat some boxes aside and placed a few on the driveway to deal with later. He noticed Josh and Rachel approaching the garage.

Josh called from the edge of the driveway. "Hey, Mr. Stan."

Stanley waved a greeting and replied, "Wasn't sure you were going to show."

Josh answered, "You said you needed help."

"Yeah," Stanley said. "I just didn't think you were serious."

Josh shrugged, dismissed Stanley's comments, and asked, "So, what are we doing today?"

"Well," Stanley replied as he surveyed the scene in the garage. "We need to go through all of these boxes and see what's in them. Then we'll decide what to get rid of and what to keep."

Josh nodded and agreed. "OK."

As Stanley and Josh began looking into boxes and sorting the contents, Rachel walked over to Cooper and began to play. As she started to pet Cooper, he broke away from her and trotted to the back of the garage, picked up a beat-up ball, and returned to Rachel with the ball in his mouth.

Stanley stared in disbelief. He was clearly surprised by Cooper's actions.

Stanley declared, "Would you look at that."

Josh looked up but couldn't see anything out of the ordinary and asked, "What?"

Cooper dropped the ball at Rachel's feet. She promptly set her rag doll aside, pounced on the ball, picked it up, and threw it for Cooper to fetch. Cooper dutifully raced after the ball.

Both Stanley and Josh stared at the scene open-mouthed.

Stanley exclaimed, "He hasn't brought that ball out in…years"

Stanley thought of how Cooper and Eddy used to play fetch with that same ball for hours at a time.

Josh looked at Rachel and cried, "Wow!"

Stanley asked, "What?"

Josh pointed at Rachel and answered, "It's Rachel. She's never let go of that doll. Miss Esther even has to put it in a plastic bag when she takes a bath."

Stanley and Josh looked on in amazement as Cooper returned with the ball, dropped it at Rachel's feet, and she promptly threw it again.

Stanley muttered to himself, "Way to go, Coop."

Stanley and Josh resumed their task of sorting through boxes. Then he turned when he heard rustling paper, and Josh giggle. Josh was looking at pictures she had found in one of the boxes.

Stanley asked defensively, "What are you laughing at?"

Josh held up one of the photos and said, "This picture."

Stanley saw her holding up a picture of him in high school, wearing a suit jacket with wide lapels and sporting a mullet haircut.

Stanley feigned annoyance saying, "Hey, you hush up." Then he chuckled and continued, "That was the style in those days."

Josh laughed and asked, "So, is this in the keep pile or the throw away pile?"

Stanley considered it for a moment, then said, "Unfortunately, keep."

Stanley picked up one of the boxes and moved it into the orderly row he had started along the wall.

Josh looked into another box and asked, "Mr. Stan?"

Stanley peered at her and answered encouragingly, "Yes."

Josh thought for a minute and spoke solemnly. "I was thinking...about what we talked about yesterday. I want to change my wish."

Stanley was intrigued. "OK." He asked, "What would you like to change it to?"

Josh answered confidently, "I was thinking about what is really important to me. I would wish for a family...like you and Mrs. Stan have."

Stanley was taken by surprise and asked incredulously, "Like what?"

Josh explained as if it was the most obvious thing in the world. "Like you have. I mean look at all you have. You have a beautiful house, a great dog, nice neighbors." She put extra emphasis on *nice neighbors* as she completed her thought. "You have everything anyone could want."

Stanley was dumbfounded. This had been the farthest thought from his mind.

He finally stammered, "I guess I hadn't considered it that way."

Josh continued to justify her position, stating, "Your wife works so you can play all day. Yeah, the way I see it, you've got it made."

Stanley stood motionless, just contemplating Josh's words and the images they invoked. Josh was oblivious to the impact of her comments, so she continued digging into the boxes.

Stanley looked at his house and thought about all it represented. Then he looked on as Rachel continued to play fetch with Cooper.

Josh reached for the next box that was labeled *Eddy's Things*. She opened the flaps on the box to reveal a new kid-sized baseball glove laying on top of other items. She pulled the glove out and put it on.

Josh was reveling in the thought of a new baseball glove. She had been embarrassed by her old glove. It didn't fit right anymore and was completely worn out. She thought how great it would be to have a glove like this one to show everybody on the team.

Josh imagined catching a line drive or scooping up a ground ball with this brand-new glove.

She exclaimed, "Aw, man. A Rawlings QS 436. This is awesome!"

Josh had been through a lot of trial and tribulation in her short life. She had bounced from one family to another hoping that she could land somewhere where she belonged. She was beginning to feel secure as she had Miss Esther to live with, and she had Rachel to take care of.

As she stood in Stanley Walters' garage amid the boxes, enjoying the feel of a new baseball glove, Josh thought things couldn't get much better. She couldn't have been more wrong.

CHAPTER 19

Stanley's anger and rage boiled and spilled over as he caught sight of Josh playing casually with Eddy's prized baseball glove.

Stanley shouted angrily, "Put that away now!"

Josh was oblivious and asked, "Why? This is great. Can I use it?"

Stanley's tone became ominous and even threatening. "No! Give that to me now!"

Stanley took two long strides toward Josh and snatched the glove off of her hand. This startled Josh, and she cowered like a whipped pup.

Stanley towered over her with an expression of rage plastered on his face.

He scolded, "You don't just take things that aren't yours."

Stanley examined the glove carefully and then lovingly placed it back in the box and began to close the flaps.

Josh's anger and frustration flared.

She shouted, "Oh yeah? Well, you don't have to yell at me. That's not how to treat someone, ya know."

Stanley stood his ground and responded, "You just need to keep out of this box."

Josh stamped her foot and began walking out of the garage as she railed, "You don't yell at people like that. And you don't hit people, either."

Stanley was taken aback by the anger in Josh's voice and confused by her reference to hitting. He stammered, "Wha… Hit? I didn't…"

Josh continued. "I thought you were my friend. You don't treat your friends like that."

Stanley was speechless.

Josh looked toward Rachel and called, "Come on, Rachel. Let's go."

Josh stalked away down the driveway with Rachel following in her wake.

Josh continued loudly. "You don't act like that. You don't hurt your friends."

As Rachel hurried to catch up, Cooper followed her out of the garage.

Stanley snapped his fingers and called, "Coop, stay here."

Cooper looked at Stanley, then back toward the retreating girls. He seemed to contemplate for a moment and then trotted after Josh and Rachel.

Stanley called louder, "Cooper, come. Now!"

Cooper ignored him and disappeared around the front of the house. Stanley was left all alone in the midst of the mess in his garage.

Stanley muttered to himself, "Stupid dog."

Just when Stanley had thought he was doing better, he unloaded on a helpless kid.

Stanley surveyed the clutter in his garage and looked at all of the boxes filled with mementos from his past. It seemed to him like he was blaming everyone else for all that had gone wrong in his life.

Then this weird character, Charles, had shown up, and Stanley had started to think about believing again. His writing had even been going fairly well, and he felt a glimmer of hope and anticipation about his career.

Stanley contemplated the fact that just when everything seemed to be going better, and he was climbing out of the deep hole he had fallen into, one random act had triggered everything in his mind. Without thinking, he had lashed out at Josh and slid all the way back down to the bottom of his pit of depression.

Lisa was unaware of the events at home, so she was still filled with hope in the aftermath of recent events. She and Deb had just finished working out in the Pilates studio, and they were toweling the sweat from their faces.

Deb was trying to get a handle on all of the exciting things Lisa had shared with her.

Deb said, "OK, let me get this straight. He started cleaning the garage?"

Lisa nodded emphatically and confirmed, "Yes."

Deb continued questioning. "And he is writing again?"

Lisa nodded again and verified, "Yes."

Deb was confused and observed, "You don't seem very happy about this."

Lisa sighed and spoke. "I don't know what to think. I mean, I have wanted this for the past two years. But to be honest, it scares me."

Deb shrugged and asked, "Scares you?"

Lisa explained, "Yes. He can be so angry. I want him to be better, and I want to help him, but I'm afraid I'm gonna screw it up and just make it worse."

Deb asked, "How could you make it worse?"

Lisa answered, "It's hard to explain. I see him making progress, and I want to be part of it; but whenever I try to help or talk with him, he just shuts me out and yells at me."

Deb gazed at Lisa sympathetically and asked, "So, what are you going to do?"

Lisa looked and felt as if she had the weight of the world on her shoulders as she admitted, "I don't know."

At that moment, Stanley was in his home office, sitting in front of the computer. He wanted to forget the horrible scene with Josh and try to get in touch with something positive again.

He typed his thoughts, feelings, and questions without mentally editing them. Words began to flow onto the screen. Stanley could have been there a few moments or a few hours. He was oblivious to his surroundings.

Finally, when he had reached a stopping point, he went back and looked through what was on the computer screen. It read: *FAMILY. Is family more valuable than money? Some would say it is.* There were surprisingly orderly paragraphs below that seemed to capture Stanley's hopes, dreams, and intentions.

He sat back in his chair and nodded in satisfaction.

He reached for his water glass on the desk but noticed it was empty. He picked up the glass and headed for the kitchen to get some water. Cooper trailed behind him.

In the kitchen, Stanley filled his glass at the sink and drank. He gazed out the kitchen window and could clearly see the mess in the garage. Deep inside, Stanley knew what he had to do.

He walked out the back door and headed for the garage. He wasn't sure he could make anything better, but—on the other hand—Stanley was convinced that things couldn't get much worse.

CHAPTER 20

Stanley's mind was made up. It was time to start doing things differently. He knew the only chance that existed to make things better involved changing the way things were. He thought how frightening change always seemed, but compared to living the life they had been living, the fear of change seemed insignificant.

Stanley strode resolutely into the garage, found the box labeled *Eddy's Things*, opened it, and peered inside. There lay Eddy's prized baseball glove and all it represented. Stanley thought how many memories were attached to that one piece of leather, but as priceless as the memories were, they represented the past, and Stanley knew he had to find a way to live in the present and on into the future.

He reached in, took out the glove, folded it over, and put it in his back pocket. Without looking back, he walked out of the garage and headed for Miss Esther's house.

Stanley had never felt comfortable around Miss Esther and her brood of foster kids, but he thought that if he was going to turn over a new leaf, he might as well turn over several leaves at the same time.

Stanley walked up on the porch and knocked on Miss Esther's door. Austin eventually ambled to the door, opened it, and stared blankly at Stanley.

Stanley realized a greeting from Austin was not going to be forthcoming, so Stanley stammered, "Uh, hi. Is Esther here?"

Austin continued to stare blankly and eventually grunted, turned, and walked away, leaving Stanley standing alone on the porch.

A few moments later, which seemed like an eternity, Miss Esther finally came to the door and looked out at Stanley. Stanley could tell instantly from her expression that Miss Esther was not at all pleased to see him.

She spoke formally in clipped tones. "Hello, Mr. Walters. May I help you?"

"Hi, Esther." Stanley inquired, "Do you think I could speak with Josh?"

Miss Esther replied sternly, "With all due respect, I don't think it is a good idea for you to talk with her anymore."

Stanley sighed in frustration and admitted, "I know. I'm sorry. I lost my temper."

Miss Esther explained, "You have to understand Josh's past. She doesn't know how to process anger."

Stanley nodded and said, "I know I crossed the line. If I could, I would really like to talk with her."

Miss Esther shrugged noncommittally and announced, "Well, she's not here now."

Stanley looked down defeatedly and said, "Oh, OK. I understand."

He turned to walk away.

Miss Esther watched Stanley's retreating back, and she stepped out onto the porch.

She called after him. "You know, it's a nice day for a walk, Stanley. Maybe you should take a walk down by the ball field."

Stanley paused in confusion momentarily, then turned, got a smile on his face, and said, "Thanks, Esther."

Miss Esther warned, "Now don't you go making a fool out of me."

Stanley assured her, "I won't. I promise."

Stanley walked the now-familiar route to the park and headed directly for the ball field. He walked around the front of the field by the visitors' bench.

Josh immediately saw Stanley approaching, and she turned away.

Cody was sitting in the bleachers next to Rachel with Cooper on her other side. Cooper just stared at Stanley noncommittally. Alex looked over and gave Stanley the evil eye as Josh was coming off the field.

Stanley called to her. "Hey, Josh. Can I talk to you for a second?"

Josh glared at Stanley, and she turned toward Alex. Alex continued defiantly to give Stanley the evil eye. Josh shrugged and warily began to walk toward Stanley. Alex turned up the heat, giving Stanley the two-fingers-to-the-eyes I'm-watching-you gesture.

Stanley was uneasy as Josh approached him from the other side of the fence. As she neared, he squatted down so he would be at her level.

Josh glared at Stanley through the chain link fence and blurted, "Make it quick. I need to get back to practice."

Stanley spoke quietly and sincerely. "Listen, Josh. I know what I did was wrong. I lost my temper, and there is no excuse for that."

Josh just looked at the ground between her and Stanley. She didn't feel like giving him a break.

Alex continued to look on from the near distance. She called, "Come on, Josh. You're up."

Josh mumbled, "I gotta go," as she turned to walk away.

Stanley pleaded desperately. "Josh, wait. Please."

She stopped, turned, and looked back at Stanley impatiently.

"This is really important," Stanley offered. "Please let me finish."

Josh reluctantly walked back toward the fence.

Stanley spoke quickly, not wanting to lose the chance to reach out to her. "OK, I'll cut to the chase. I lost my temper, and I was wrong. Can you please forgive me?"

Josh looked directly into his face and stared into his eyes.

Stanley was bewildered and asked, "What?"

Josh explained, "I just need to see into your eyes."

Stanley asked, "My eyes? Why?"

Josh answered matter-of-factly, "To make sure you're not lying."

Josh continued to stare into Stanley's eyes for a long moment.

Stanley awaited her verdict and asked, "Well?"

The ice cracked slightly between them, and Josh admitted, "You're doing all right."

She smiled a little.

Stanley returned her smile, nodded, and said, "Good."

Stanley stood up from his crouch and grasped the fence that separated them. He had heard a wise man once explain that in order to receive forgiveness, you've got to be willing to give it away. Stanley had never known how hard that was. He knew he needed a way to keep Eddy's memory alive while not living in the past.

Just then, Stanley understood that the only true and meaningful tribute to Eddy's life was to move forward and take his memory along.

Chapter 21

No temple or courtroom was ever a place of forgiveness or resolution more than the ball field in the park that day. Time seemed to stand still as Stanley and Josh stood and looked at one another through the fence that surrounded the baseball diamond. Stanley and Josh both needed to find a place inside themselves to trust enough to accept and offer forgiveness.

The trust seemed to build between them as Stanley broke the silence and announced, "Here. I want you to have something."

Stanley reached behind him and pulled the glove out of his back pocket.

A broad grin broke out on Josh's face as she saw it. It was hard for her to believe what was happening.

She asked, "For real?"

Josh ran toward the end of the fence so she could get around to the other side where Stanley stood. The whole team had lined up along the edge of the field and looked on as Josh approached Stanley.

He finally noticed that the whole team was watching, so he smiled and waved. One of the players returned the wave.

Alex was still not totally convinced that Stanley was on the level. She glared at the player who had waved and punched him in the arm.

As Josh approached Stanley, he held the glove out toward her. She took it, put it on, and smiled up at Stanley. As he returned her smile, he watched her run back around the end of the fence and rejoin her teammates. Stanley walked to the end of the fence.

Josh stopped just before she reached her teammates. She turned abruptly and returned to Stanley. She reached up to him. Stanley bent down, and Josh kissed him on the cheek.

Josh beamed and said gratefully, "Thank you, Mr. Stan."

Josh raced back toward her teammates holding out her new glove for everyone to see. Alex and the rest of the team were all buzzing with excitement as their star pitcher had a new glove and maybe a new friend.

Stanley stood alone watching the scene play out before him. He couldn't stop smiling, and he felt that somehow a weight had been lifted from him.

Then, unexpectedly, all other sounds seemed to fall away, and Stanley could distinctly, inexplicably hear the sound of a beating heart. He reached up and put his hand on his chest over his heart. Somehow, he knew it was his own heartbeat.

Stanley watched Josh and the other players going through their normal practice routine.

Sam approached Stanley and said, "It does a heart good to help heal another person."

Stanley turned to Sam, smiled, and agreed. "More than you know, Sam. More than you know."

Stanley enjoyed the rest of the afternoon in the park. The grass seemed greener, the sky seemed bluer, and the joy of watching the kids practice baseball was beyond anything he had previously experienced in all the years he had coached.

As the sun slowly drifted into the western sky and the kids' practice broke up with everyone picking up equipment and heading home, Stanley walked away from the baseball field.

He hadn't gone far when Cooper joined him. They paused for a brief reunion as Stanley petted Cooper, and Cooper enthusiastically licked his hand. All seemed right with the world as Stanley and Cooper walked out of the park and headed for home.

Stanley felt that a day like this deserved a special celebration.

When Lisa drove into the driveway after a long day at work, she wasn't sure what to expect at home. Recently, she never knew if she would find Stanley silent and depressed or raging with anger.

The light from the house seemed to glow from the windows as she approached the front door. As she entered, Lisa noticed that the living room was immaculate. Wonderful smells were emanating from the kitchen, and the table was formally set for two.

There was a vase of flowers placed at the center of the table, and candles were burning brightly. The lamp was prominently placed on the table as well.

Lisa followed the aroma of great food into the kitchen where she saw Stanley with an apron around his waist and a hand towel tossed over his shoulder.

Several pots were on the stove. One of them was boiling with noodles in it. Ingredients were spread throughout the kitchen. Stanley was humming to himself as he dipped his finger into another pot on the stove that held a red sauce. He tasted it and nodded in approval.

Lisa was stunned by the scene. She cleared her throat to get his attention. "Ahem."

Stanley was startled. He whirled quickly and said, "Oh, hey. I didn't hear you come in. Um, dinner will be ready in a minute. Why don't you go get changed."

Lisa just stood there, staring at the scene dumbfounded.

Stanley approached her, gently grasped her by the shoulders, and turned her toward the door, saying, "Go on."

Lisa left the kitchen with feelings of surprise, joy, and anticipation. Stanley quickly turned back to his culinary labors.

As Lisa changed clothes and prepared for what she hoped would be a very special evening, Stanley put the final touches on their celebration dinner. There was spaghetti with red sauce, garlic bread, and salad, and Stanley was just pouring the wine as Lisa joined him in the dining room wearing a dress he hadn't seen in several years.

The couple sat down together at the table, experiencing feelings that they had not felt in their home since before the tragedy. They both knew they could never recapture what had been between them before, but something new and exciting was blooming in their lives.

CHAPTER 22

There are times when a familiar place can seem so comfortable and normal that it is simply overlooked; and then there are times when one can experience the most extraordinary event within an ordinary or normal setting.

Like millions of couples that same evening, Stanley and Lisa were eating dinner together, in their dining room, inside their average home, in their normal neighborhood; but that night, among all nights, was special.

Lisa looked at the beautiful flowers on the table that Stanley had picked from their own yard. They were highlighted by the soft glow of the candles, and the whole setting seemed magical.

Lisa spoke in disbelief. "Stanley, I don't know what to say here. This is amazing."

Stanley responded, "Lisa, before you say anything, I really need to say something to you."

Lisa gazed at him intently.

Stanley continued, "This whole thing with Charles and the believing that things can be different. It has got me thinking. Then with Josh…"

Lisa was confused. She interrupted, asking, "Josh? From next door?"

Stanley nodded and explained, "Yeah. I hired her to help me clean the garage."

Lisa still seemed confused as Stanley forged ahead, saying, "Well, we were talking, and she said something that took me by surprise." Stanley paused to collect his thoughts and then continued, "She said if she could have anything she wanted in life, it would be to have a family… just like you and me."

Lisa wasn't sure how to take that and asked, "Are we a family?"

Stanley spoke solemnly. "Lisa, I really want us to be."

Lisa was struggling with what she was hearing.

She tried to put her thoughts and feelings into words, saying, "Stanley, I really want to believe you, but…"

Lisa was overwhelmed with emotion and unable to continue.

Stanley tried to recover the moment and offered, "Listen. Something incredible happened today. I gave Eddy's baseball glove to Josh."

Lisa couldn't believe what she was hearing as she knew what that glove had meant to Eddy and what it represented to Stanley.

"You did?"

Stanley nodded and explained excitedly. "It's something I knew I needed to do. When I did... You're never going to believe this."

Lisa didn't know where this was heading but knew that it was something vitally important to Stanley. She reached across the table and held his hand as he shared his experience, saying, "I actually heard the sound of my heartbeat. I know it sounds strange, but I could actually hear it."

Emotion flooded over Lisa.

She said, "Stanley, I can hardly believe what you are saying."

Stanley tried to gather his thoughts and deal with everything that had happened that day. It was hard to make sense of it all, but he knew he had to share it.

He admitted, "Honey, you were right. For the last two years, the thing I feared the most was letting go. As if doing that was wrong. But when I gave Josh that glove... When I did, I felt a sense of peace come over me. I haven't felt that in a long time. I feel like everything is different now. I'm so sorry for the way I've been."

Lisa stared into Stanley's eyes for a long moment, daring to believe what she had heard. For the first time in two years, Lisa was sitting face to face with the man she knew and loved. She leaned toward Stanley, and they kissed.

The couple talked animatedly as they enjoyed the rest of their dinner. In some ways, they felt as if they were getting reacquainted, and in other ways, they were revisiting old, familiar places together.

The next morning, Lisa awoke well-rested, energized, and excited to meet the new day. One glance beside her told her that Stanley's side of the bed had been slept in. She smiled with satisfaction and got out of bed.

Stanley had gotten up early and left the house quickly that day as he wanted to get to the ball field before the team started to practice.

As Stanley and Cooper rushed across the park toward the baseball diamond, the coach was just unloading the equipment and trying to organize the team. The players looked on as Stanley spoke privately to the coach for a moment. Then the coach gave Stanley a Tigers baseball hat and a coach's whistle. Stanley and the coach shook hands. Stanley looked excited, and the coach seemed relieved.

Josh ran up to Stanley and gave him a big hug.

That night, Josh and Rachel joined Stanley and Lisa for dinner in the Walters' home. Lisa listened excitedly as Stanley and Josh told baseball stories, recounting all the events of that day's practice.

Rachel secretly slipped Cooper some food under the table.

Lisa couldn't help but consider how the changes in Stanley, along with the presence of the two girls, made their sad house seem like a happy home. She had barely known Josh and Rachel even though they were living in Miss Esther's house and she saw them around the neighborhood every day.

It was apparent to Lisa that Rachel had gone through a horrible ordeal. Beyond the fact that she wouldn't or couldn't talk, there were the angry burn scars on her arm and the charred rag doll she had to have with her at all times.

Josh, Lisa knew, had been abused and neglected for most of her life. She had been shuffled from foster home to foster home and from institution to institution so much that she never felt safe and secure anywhere.

With all of the dysfunction and turmoil that Stanley and Lisa had been through in their own lives, it was amazing that the four of them could somehow come together around the dinner table and everything seem so normal and natural.

With all of the miracles going on around her, Lisa wondered what else might be possible. She couldn't wait to find out.

CHAPTER 23

Stanley woke early the next day and realized that, for the first time in months, he had made it through the night without being forced to endure the reoccurring dream of the worst day of his life.

Stanley slipped out of bed so as not to wake Lisa. He looked down at her sleeping form and thought how lucky he was that she had patiently stuck with him over the past few years.

Stanley rushed down the hallway to the office as he couldn't wait to begin writing the accounts of all his experiences and the thoughts that went along with them.

He felt he'd only been working a few minutes, but when Lisa came in to offer him some iced tea, Stanley realized it was already mid-morning.

Lisa asked, "How's it going?"

Stanley looked away from his computer screen and glanced toward Lisa, saying, "I think I've figured out what my last wish is."

Lisa asked, "Yeah, what?"

Stanley stated confidently, "To love what I do."

Lisa nodded her head in agreement and left Stanley to continue his writing. He was in a productive, creative flow, the likes of which he had never experienced.

Later that same afternoon, Stanley was on the phone with his literary agent. Stanley excitedly explained what he had been doing and all of the things he had written about his experiences.

His agent had nearly given up on Stanley. Years before, Stanley had been one of his better clients, but over the past couple of years, there had been an ongoing series of disappointments, missed deadlines, and excuses.

The agent couldn't believe that somehow Stanley was totally transformed. It was like the old Stanley Walters, but even better.

Stanley's literary agent gave him a lot of positive feedback and some prominent people for him to call on to get interviews for the new book project.

As the agent spoke, Stanley scribbled notes on a pad. He wrote: Interview with Steve Forbes. November 3. 2:30 P.M.. Set up meeting with Paula Marshall and Harland Stonecipher.

Stanley couldn't believe what he was hearing as his literary agent opened the floodgates of his publisher's contacts. Before he knew it, Stanley had access to a veritable Who's Who of celebrities and high profile, successful people.

Stanley bounded into his publisher's office and was greeted with excitement and enthusiasm by everyone he ran into. The whole team was thrilled about Stanley's new book project.

His publisher shook his hand vigorously and said, "Stanley, we are proud to have you back on the team."

Stanley rushed home excitedly and called every one of his creditors that had been hounding him. He apologized to them all for the delay and made arrangements to get everyone paid in full.

His excitement for his reemerging career was equaled by the joy he felt coaching again.

It was a beautiful day as Josh was pitching, and Stanley was hitting the ball so that the team could practice their fielding. Josh wound up and threw her best fast ball. Stanley felt like he was a teenager again on the high school baseball team. He swung with all his might and connected solidly. The ball rocketed high into the air and soared over the outfield, clearing the fence by a great distance.

There was a handsome jogger plodding his way around the park just as Stanley's homerun blast came back to earth. Stanley started to yell, warning the jogger, but it was too late. The ball hit him squarely atop the head. Stanley and the whole team raced out to check on the jogger; but within a few minutes, he was revived and seemed almost back to normal.

In the coming days, Stanley and Lisa developed a closeness they had never known before. They enjoyed spending time together, and they arranged several outings in the park that included Miss Esther and all of her kids. Josh and Rachel particularly enjoyed these extended-family outings.

Although it had been a long time coming, Stanley's garage-cleaning project finally appeared as if it might get completed. On one of the last days they were working in the garage, Josh and Rachel were bewildered as Stanley found his bicycle pump that he thought they had stolen. He laughed aloud.

Stanley focused intensely on his book project. He took a whirlwind trip to New York for a meeting with Steve Forbes. Stanley had always been an admirer of Forbes and couldn't wait to get his input for the book.

As Mr. Forbes' limousine delivered Stanley to the Forbes Building, Stanley told the chauffeur, "Thank you for the ride. I've never been in a limo before, and you've been most gracious."

The limo driver smiled as he opened the door and said, "Don't worry. I'll see you again after your meeting. Mr. Forbes insists on the round-trip treatment."

Stanley looked up toward the top of the Forbes Building and then glanced around at all of the skyscrapers that dotted the New York cityscape.

Inside the building, everyone—including Mr. Forbes—treated Stanley with respect, and they all seemed genuinely interested in his book. Stanley had to pinch himself to make sure this was really happening to him as he spent an uninterrupted half hour with Steve Forbes in the ornate library that Steve's father, Malcolm Forbes, had built into the Forbes Building.

Stanley felt like he was floating on air as he excitedly rushed out of the Forbes Building after the interview. He couldn't believe the transformation that was taking place in his world. He wasn't sure if it all had started with Josh, Charles, Lisa, or maybe when he decided to let go of the past and just believe.

CHAPTER 24

As the plane lifted off from New York taking Stanley back home, he couldn't wait to tell Lisa about everything that had happened and was happening.

As he arrived home and rushed into the house, Lisa was in the kitchen preparing dinner. Stanley hurried in, still carrying his coat and briefcase.

As Stanley set down all of his things in one of the kitchen chairs, Lisa spoke excitedly. "So, how did it go? Tell me everything."

"It went great," Stanley recounted with enthusiasm. "He loved the book idea and the title *Just Believe*. He is going to help me get more interviews with other successful people."

Lisa smiled broadly and said, "Stanley, I am so proud of you!"

Lisa walked over to Stanley and gave him a big hug. Both of them could feel the excitement of the day, the promise of tomorrow, and the fact that they were—once again—a couple.

Stanley voiced what was on both of their minds. "You know, Charles returns tomorrow."

Lisa handed Stanley a plate of food and said, "It doesn't seem like it's been 30 days."

Stanley nodded in agreement.

The couple sat at the kitchen table and enjoyed their dinner together.

For the rest of the evening, they talked about all of the exciting things going on in their life together. The only topic that seemed to be avoided was the pending return of Charles.

The next morning, everything in the Walters' home appeared normal and like any other day, except Stanley and Lisa were sitting in their living room staring at the lamp on the coffee table.

Stanley glanced toward Lisa then back at the lamp and said, "So, what do we do? Are we supposed to say something?"

Lisa shrugged and replied, "I don't know."

Stanley said with a chuckle and an ironic smile, "Maybe I should get a hammer."

Lisa gave Stanley a sidelong look, letting him know she wasn't ready yet to see the humor in the fact that he had temporarily destroyed the lamp with his hammer.

Lisa picked up the lamp and stared at it intently. She read the inscription on the side. "Hmm. *Just Believe*. I think I do."

Suddenly they heard a noise coming from their kitchen.

Stanley turned to Lisa and asked, "Was that the toaster?"

Stanley and Lisa just stared at one another, then rose in unison and hurried into the kitchen. They were greeted with the sight of Charles calmly buttering a piece of toast as if he belonged there. A hot cup of coffee was on the counter next to Charles.

As he heard them enter, Charles turned and said casually, "Oh, good morning."

Stanley and Lisa were still in awe of Charles, and they mumbled together, "Good morning."

As Charles picked up his toast and coffee and moved toward the table, he announced, "I can't tell you how excited I am to hear about your wishes."

Stanley and Lisa joined Charles at the kitchen table. He took a bite of his toast and a sip of the coffee.

"Ahhhh," he declared. "Now that's good."

As Stanley and Lisa simply sat and watched Charles, he said, "Now, then. Let's hear those wishes. What have you got?"

Stanley and Lisa fell silent and looked at one another sheepishly as Charles stared at them with great anticipation.

When the silence became uncomfortable, Stanley tried to explain. "Well, Charles. You see...we...Lisa and I...well, we, um..."

Charles motioned for him to continue and said expectantly, "Yes..."

Lisa took the lead and said, "I think what Stanley is trying to say is that we don't...well...we don't have any wishes."

Charles sat up straight in surprise and spoke animatedly. "Don't have any wishes? Well, how can this be? If I remember correctly, you asked me for three wishes."

Stanley nodded and replied, "Well, we had wishes, but they kind of got answered on their own."

"Most fascinating," Charles prompted. "Do tell."

Lisa offered an explanation. "Well, our first wish was to have lots of money. Well, that kinda happened."

Charles interrupted and questioned, "It happened?"

He seemed a bit perplexed as he took out a small notebook and started paging through it.

Charles declared, "I don't remember authorizing any wishes in regard to money."

Stanley jumped in, saying, "No, no. It's not like that. It was because of the third wish."

Charles was baffled and asked, "The third wish?"

"You see," Stanley offered, "I wanted to do something I loved, so that was going to be my third wish. And then I got this idea for a book. Yeah, it just came to me. You'll love the title."

Stanley and Lisa looked at one another.

Stanley nodded, and Lisa announced, *"Just Believe."*

Charles let out a hearty laugh and declared, "Well, I'll be."

"Yeah," Stanley continued. "I pitched the idea to my publisher, and he flipped over it. I got the largest advance for a book in the publisher's history. So, that took care of wish number one. And well, wish number three."

Charles was thoughtful as he listened intently. He closed the notebook, put it back in his pocket, and took another sip of his coffee.

Charles was eager to hear the rest and prompted, "Go on. What about wish number two?"

"Well." Stanley shared his thoughts. "Wish number two just kind of happened on its own. It took a child to show me what I needed. My second wish was for a happy family."

Stanley looked lovingly toward Lisa, reached out, and held her hand.

Charles said, "Let me guess. You already had it. You just couldn't see it."

Stanley thought about it for a moment, then looked directly at Charles and said in agreement, "Exactly. It was there all the time. I just didn't believe it anymore."

Charles took another bite of his toast and a final sip of coffee. He leaned forward and looked at the couple intently as he spoke. "Stanley, Lisa, I am so happy to hear that you have grasped the essence of this message. You see, most people go through life not understanding that they have been given this amazing gift. Each one of us has the ability to create the life we want. We just need to believe we can. This is a truth that has been passed down through the ages, and now the two of you have taken hold of it."

Charles gave them a big smile and continued. "Now the question is: What will you do with this truth? Keep it to yourselves, or share it with others?"

Lisa smiled in understanding, but Stanley wasn't totally onboard yet.

He asked, "Share it with others?"

Charles nodded and said, "Yes, Stanley. Now that you know the truth, you need to share it with others."

Stanley glanced toward Lisa and then looked back at Charles.

Charles said, "When the time is right, you will know what to do. I believe in you."

Charles smiled at them both then declared, "Well, I best be on my way. I have quite the report to write."

Charles rose and casually walked toward the door. He opened it, bowed slightly toward Stanley and Lisa, then walked out. Stanley and Lisa sat staring at one another, still not totally believing what they had seen.

Stanley questioned, "That's it? He just walks out the door?"

Suddenly, the light bulb in the kitchen ceiling grew brighter and brighter. Then it popped loudly. Lisa screamed.

CHAPTER 25

Lisa was excited about all of the changes taking place in Stanley, his career, and their life together. She couldn't seem to stay away from the home office. It had been a place of despair and failure, but in the past few days, it seemed to have been transformed.

As she walked down the hallway, she could see that Cooper was lying on the floor in the doorway to the office. Lisa walked right up to him, but he didn't move. Cooper just laid still and stared up at Lisa as if he were protecting a secret.

Lisa motioned and said, "Come on, Coop. Out of the way."

Cooper just continued to lay motionless and stare up at her.

She implored, "Cooper, I gotta go."

Cooper remained still and filled with resolve.

Lisa tried to justify her intentions as she explained, "Don't look at me like that. I'm not doing anything wrong. He doesn't care if I read it."

Cooper tilted his head to the side as he continued to stare at her. Lisa knew that Cooper wasn't buying her story.

She waved dismissively and said, "Ahhh, never mind."

She turned and walked on down the hallway, saying over her shoulder, "You know, you're no saint. I remember a little puppy that chewed up Daddy's new phone case. Did I tell on you? Nooooo."

As Lisa walked out the front door, Cooper stood up and scurried away from his post guarding the office. He knew his work was done there for the day.

Lisa walked down the driveway and entered the garage where Stanley was standing at the workbench.

Lisa greeted him, "Hey, there."

Stanley turned to face her and echoed, "Hey."

Lisa said, "I'll pick up the new uniforms on my way home tonight."

Stanley answered enthusiastically. "They are going to be so excited. I'm glad we got them in time. This is the biggest game of the season."

Lisa agreed. They're going to look great. "See ya later."

Lisa kissed Stanley and hurried out of the garage.

Stanley watched Lisa retreating down the driveway and was thinking how lucky he was when he noticed a commotion in Miss Esther's yard.

All of Miss Esther's kids and Alex were gathered around Josh. Josh was covered with dirt and had scrapes on her cheek and on her arm.

Stanley left the garage and walked over to the kids to find out what in the world was going on. He realized he was developing protective and loving feelings toward Josh.

Stanley called, "Josh, what happened to you?"

Alex explained, "She just kicked Ronny Martin's butt!"

The kids all laughed, but Josh seemed embarrassed, and Stanley was concerned. Josh was trying to brush the dirt off herself and clean herself up.

Stanley asked, "What…? What happened?"

Alex recounted the story. "Well, Ronny called Cody a freak, and Josh told him to shut up. And then Ronny said to make him…"

Josh appeared nervous, obviously not wanting Alex to tell the story, but Alex continued.

"…so…she did."

The kids all laughed again.

Stanley looked at Josh and asked, "You OK, Josh?"

Josh nodded solemnly.

Cody offered details with enthusiasm. "You should have seen her. She was like a cage fighter."

Miss Esther hurried out of her house and approached the kids. It was obvious to everyone that she was not happy. The group fell silent.

Miss Esther called, "Josh, what have you done?"

Josh tried to defend herself. "He started it."

Miss Esther took charge and commanded, "Go in the house, and get cleaned up."

Josh headed for the house.

Miss Esther turned toward Alex and spoke sternly. "Alex, it's probably a good idea for you to go home now."

Alex walked away, and all of Miss Esther's kids went into the house except Rachel who picked up Cooper's ball and threw it. Cooper dutifully raced after the ball and brought it back.

Miss Esther turned toward Stanley and spoke softly. "That poor girl."

Stanley asked, "What's the problem?"

Miss Esther explained. "She is really having a hard time with all of this."

Stanley didn't understand and asked, "All of what?"

Miss Esther looked directly at Stanley and stated, "She is being adopted."

Stanley was incredulous. He blurted, "Adopted?"

Miss Esther nodded and said, "Yes. She's had several visits with a prospective family.

Stanley was in shock.

He blurted, "She's leaving? She hasn't said a word."

Miss Esther nodded and said, "That doesn't surprise me. She doesn't want to go."

Stanley sighed and asked, "How soon is this going to happen?"

Miss Esther shrugged and answered, "I'm not sure. Could be any time now. Depends on how the visits go."

Stanley was in shock. He muttered, "Wow. I never expected that."

Miss Esther's gaze fell as she explained, "What makes this more difficult is that they don't want to adopt Rachel."

Stanley spoke defiantly. "What? They have to! Those two need each other."

They both fell silent for a moment. Stanley felt sick. Esther could sense that the news had hit him hard.

She offered, "I think the thing she is most upset about is leaving you."

Stanley looked intently at Esther and said, "I can't believe she is leaving."

Rachel continued to play. She was oblivious to the conversation going on between Miss Esther and Stanley and all it represented.

Cooper brought the ball back to her and dropped it at her feet. Rachel threw it again, and it bounced off of the house and began bounding down the driveway.

Cooper raced after the ball. Rachel could see that the ball was headed for the street with Cooper in pursuit. She looked up toward Miss Esther and Stanley, but they were engrossed in their deep conversation and didn't notice.

CHAPTER 26

Adelivery truck was moving down the street. The driver was distracted as he was talking on his cell phone and trying to read the address on his clipboard at the same time. He didn't notice the ball rolling out into the middle of the street.

Rachel was struggling with what to do. She began hurrying down the driveway as she saw the truck coming closer.

She watched Cooper dart out into the middle of the street, and then—without thinking—Rachel called out his name. "Cooper!"

Miss Esther and Stanley were stunned to hear Rachel's voice. They turned in unison and saw her running toward the street.

Rachel continued yelling, "Cooper! Cooper!"

Stanley raced toward Rachel as he could see the approaching disaster. Suddenly, the image of Rachel in the street turned into Eddy. Stanley's nightmare came to life. Stanley could see Eddy, once again, riding his bike down the driveway and into the street.

Stanley looked toward Rachel as he ran, but he yelled, "Eddy, stop!"

Rachel ignored Stanley and rushed into the street in front of the oncoming truck.

Stanley continued to rush toward Rachel, but in his mind, he saw his son.

He continued to scream, "Eddy! Eddy, stop!"

Rachel was only focused on Cooper, and she was oblivious to all else around her.

She called frantically, "Cooper!"

Stanley saw visions of Eddy's face, the truck approaching, and a bent and mangled bike lying in the middle of the street.

Rachel reached Cooper who was standing in front of the oncoming truck.

She grabbed his collar and pulled, calling, "Cooper, come on! Come on!"

As the truck bore down on them, the driver glanced up and saw a young girl right in front of him. He slammed on his brakes, and everything seemed to move forward in slow motion.

Stanley ran out into the street, right in front of the truck, and grabbed Rachel just in time.

Cooper jumped out of the way, and the truck squealed to a stop five feet past where Rachel and Cooper had been standing an instant before. The truck came to rest with its tire rolling over Cooper's ball which loudly popped.

Stanley was sitting on the curb at the edge of the street, holding a trembling child in his arms.

He saw visions of Eddy as he said soothingly, "Eddy, it's going to be OK. Hang in there, buddy. It's going to be all right."

Stanley yelled loudly, "Somebody get an ambulance!"

Then he said more softly, "Help my son."

Stanley hugged the child and was jolted back into the moment, realizing that he had been holding Rachel all the time. Stanley broke down and wept.

Miss Esther, a group of concerned neighbors, and the truck driver were all gathered around Stanley where he sat on the curb holding Rachel.

Stanley continued to cry and called plaintively, "I'm so sorry, Eddy. I'm so sorry."

Eventually, Miss Esther was able to take Rachel from Stanley and carry her back home.

Stanley slowly walked back to his own house and was seated on Eddy's bed holding the lamp when Lisa frantically rushed in, asking, "I got here as fast as I could. Are you OK?"

Stanley spoke softly. "Yeah, I'm fine."

Lisa sat next to Stanley on Eddy's bed.

She said, "Oh, Stanley. That was so scary."

Stanley turned toward Lisa with a distraught expression on his face.

Lisa asked, "What is it?"

Pain filled Stanley's voice as he announced, "I found out Josh is being adopted."

Lisa appeared crestfallen.

Stanley continued. "It feels like we're losing Eddy all over again, and there's nothing I can do about it."

Lisa and Stanley sat silently and held one another.

Stanley couldn't get Josh, Rachel, and the circumstances of the near-tragedy off his mind.

The next day he felt empty as he was simply going through the motions of his normal routine. He felt like lying down and doing nothing, but he had made the commitment to coach the kids' team, and today was the big game. The Tigers were playing their archrivals, the Sharks, who were the best team in the league.

Stanley was loading all of the equipment and the new uniforms into his car. He was looking forward to surprising everybody with the big-league-style new uniforms.

As he was arranging everything in the trunk, Miss Esther approached from next door.

Stanley grabbed one of the uniforms from the top box, held it up, and called, "Hey, Esther. Take a look at these."

The jersey he was holding up had the number seven on it. It was particularly poignant as that had been Eddy's number.

"Those are great." Miss Esther was subdued as she continued. "Stanley, I wanted to tell you something before you go."

Hearing Miss Esther's tone, Stanley was concerned and asked, "What is it?"

Miss Esther said, "This will be Josh's last game."

Stanley was shocked and asked, "Why?"

Miss Esther explained, "I just got a call this morning. The adoption is going through."

Stanley was completely deflated by this. He sat on the back bumper of the car and stared up at her.

Miss Esther continued. "There is one other thing you should know. The adoptive family wanted to come see her last game."

Stanley didn't know what to say and muttered, "Oh, OK."

Miss Esther tried to console Stanley, saying, "I'm so sorry, dear."

Stanley just stared at Esther without expression. Then he looked down at the jersey he was holding.

Stanley and Miss Esther couldn't find anything else to say. It was an awkward, heart-wrenching moment for both of them. Finally, Esther patted Stanley on the shoulder and walked back toward her house.

With all the good things that had been happening in Stanley's life, he was committed to not slipping back into his depression. He stared at the jersey with the bright, bold number 7 on it and made up his mind that if this was going to be Josh's last game, he was going to do everything a coach could do to make it the best game ever.

CHAPTER 27

When kids play baseball, there are no small games. To a 10-year-old, every outing is like the Major League All-Star game or the World Series.

To Josh and her teammates, this game was even bigger than usual. They were playing the Sharks, the best team in the league, and the Tigers had never beaten them.

There were more parents, grandparents, and friends in the stands than usual owing to the great weather and the competitive matchup.

Josh was wearing the number seven jersey that was so significant to Stanley. She would be pitching that day, so she was warming up, throwing to Alex.

Bernice—Josh's state welfare worker—and the couple who were all set to adopt Josh arrived and took a seat in the stands. Josh noticed them sitting there. Bernice and the couple smiled broadly and waved. Josh feigned a smile and returned a halfhearted wave.

Stanley watched the exchange between Josh and the adoptive couple. He glanced up in the stands where Lisa was sitting and noticed she had witnessed the same exchange. Stanley and Lisa looked at one another mournfully.

Miss Esther and her other kids arrived and sat near Bernice and Josh's prospective new parents. Deb joined Lisa in the stands, and Rachel and Cooper sat beside them.

The game was exciting and more competitive than the previous games between the two teams, but by the second inning, the visiting Sharks had already taken a 5-to-2 lead over the Tigers.

Josh was pitching well, and Alex was playing catcher and shouting encouragement to Josh from behind the plate. There was a Sharks' runner on third base, and the Tigers were trying not to let the lead grow any bigger.

Josh threw a great pitch, and the batter popped it up into the shallow outfield. The fielder got under it and was a little shaky but made the catch. The runner on third tagged up and raced for home as the outfielder threw the ball to the plate.

Alex caught it and was prepared to tag the runner out, but he went into a slide and intentionally spiked Alex in the leg. Alex cried out in pain and dropped the ball.

The umpire yelled, "Safe!"

Stanley raced toward the field from the bench and yelled to the umpire, "Come on, Blue. What's that?"

Josh was livid. She threw down her glove and stomped toward the offending base runner who had injured her best friend, Alex. Stanley saw the pending disaster and raced over to intercept Josh.

Stanley took her to the side and tried to encourage her. The adoptive couple was standing in the bleachers watching the interaction.

Stanley calmly spoke to Josh. "Hey, come here. Don't let this get to you, OK?"

Josh simply glared at Stanley as if he had done something wrong.

Stanley asked, "What's going on?"

Josh became expressionless and said, "Nothing. I'm fine."

Stanley knew something was not right, and he continued to gaze at her.

Josh repeated, "I'm fine. Let's just play."

Josh grumpily headed back to the mound and picked up her glove.

Stanley was walking back to the bench when he noticed Josh angrily kicking at the dirt on the mound. Stanley glanced into the bleachers and exchanged a look with the adoptive father. Stanley smiled politely and kept walking.

Josh began pitching with a renewed ferocity. The game went back and forth until the fourth inning when the Sharks' player who had spiked Alex came to bat. He and Alex glared at one another as he took his place in the batter's box.

Alex crouched behind the plate and pointed to her thigh as a signal to Josh. Josh nodded with a smirk, wound up, and threw her best fastball, striking the batter in the middle of his thigh. He dropped the bat and fell to the ground groaning in pain.

Josh shrugged and offhandedly said, "Oopsy doodles."

Stanley yelled at her from the bench. "Josh!"

Stanley jumped to his feet and signaled for a time out. He raced out to the mound where Josh had turned her back to him.

Stanley commanded, "Turn around and look at me."

Josh reluctantly turned around.

Stanley demanded, "Hey, what's going on?"

Josh stared at him angrily and spat out, "What do you care?"

Stanley was taken aback by her response. Josh was staring at the ground. Stanley stooped down so that he would be at her level. Lisa and the adoptive parents looked on from the bleachers.

Stanley spoke softly. "Hey, look at me."

Josh looked up at him.

Stanley asked, "What's this all about? You can beat this team."

Josh shrugged dismissively and responded, "None of this matters anyhow. After this game is over, you won't have to put up with me anymore."

Stanley didn't understand her attitude and tried to reason with her, saying, "Josh, I'm not putting up with you, I…"

Stanley was interrupted as the umpire approached the mound, calling, "Coach, play ball."

Josh turned away from Stanley. He walked back toward the bench and noticed the adoptive couple watching him from the bleachers.

The game went back and forth through the middle innings, and the Tigers rallied and mounted a comeback. Stanley noticed all of the players cheering wildly on the bench except Josh who sat alone sulking.

The Tigers tied the game. The scoreboard read 6 to 6 as the game went into the 9th inning.

Stanley realized that the game and many more important things were coming down to the wire.

CHAPTER 28

Stanley stood in front of the Tigers' bench and surveyed the players on the field. He knew that Josh and her teammates would remember this game for the rest of their lives.

Stanley recalled several of his own crucial Little League games. There were times he could smell the freshly mown grass and hear the shouts and cheers from the fans and his teammates from decades ago. More than anything else, Stanley remembered the applause and shouts of encouragement from his own mother and father.

Those images would be with him forever.

Stanley called to the umpire. "Time out."

The umpire nodded and signaled that a time-out had been granted.

Stanley motioned for the team to gather 'round him.

He spoke to them intensely. "OK, team. This is it. We've got two outs, and we only need one run to win."

Stanley paused to make eye contact with each player.

He continued. "You have all played a beautiful game against the best team in the league, and they are not going to just hand this to us."

Stanley's gaze settled on Josh as he continued speaking to the team and, especially, to her. "You know, there are things that happen in life that are out of our control. That is just the way life is. We may not be able to control what is going on around us, but we can control ourselves. We get to choose how we respond to what life throws at us. We get to choose to believe that anything is possible—even if it looks like things aren't going to happen the way we hoped they would. The question is, are you willing to believe?"

Stanley was proud of the kids.

He spoke to them each in turn. "Alex, do you believe?"

Alex spoke with conviction. "Yes."

Stanley asked, "What about you, Chris?"

Chris called loudly, "Yes."

Stanley looked at another player and questioned, "Jason?"

He answered, "Yes."

Stanley stepped back and addressed the entire team. "Tigers, do you believe?"

Every member of the team except Josh yelled in unison. "Yes!"

Stanley echoed their enthusiasm and cried, "One more time."

The team yelled at the top of their lungs, "YES!"

The Tigers jumped, clapped, yelled, and slapped one another on the back. When they finally settled, Stanley intently looked over the players. He and Josh made direct eye contact.

She asked, "Do you believe?"

Stanley answered without hesitation. "Yes, Josh. I believe in you. I will always believe in you."

Josh smiled at Stanley.

Stanley encouraged the team. "Now let's hear that Tiger roar, and go out there and win!"

The entire team, including Josh, put their hands out like claws and roared in true Tiger fashion.

Stanley announced, "Josh, you're up."

He took her aside and instructed, "Watch the inside pitch. Step back from the plate a little."

Josh nodded in understanding and said, "OK."

Stanley's gaze bore into Josh's eyes, and he reaffirmed, "I believe in you."

Josh smiled confidently, put her bat over on her shoulder, and headed for the plate.

Stanley could hear Lisa and Deb cheering enthusiastically.

Lisa called, "Come on, Josh. Knock it outta here."

Deb joined in. "Let's go, Josh. You can do it!"

Josh glanced toward Lisa and Deb and smiled. The adoptive couple looked on silently with anticipation.

As Josh stepped into the batter's box, the Sharks' catcher—Ronny Martin—said ominously, "Watch yourself, Joshy. You might get hurt."

He smacked his catcher's mitt to emphasize the point.

The pitcher wound up and threw the ball directly toward Josh. She jumped back out of the way and let the ball narrowly pass by her.

The umpire called, "Ball." Then he looked directly toward the pitcher and said sternly, "Let's keep this a friendly game."

Josh stepped back into the batter's box and up to the plate. Then she remembered Stanley's coaching and took a half step back away from the plate.

Stanley looked on from the bench and nodded in satisfaction as he said to himself, *There you go, kid.*

The pitcher wound up and threw the ball inside, but Josh was ready for it. She smacked it just over the shortstop's head, and she raced toward first base. The Sharks' outfielder made a good play, but Josh was safe on first base.

Jeff was the next Tiger batter to approach the plate. As Josh looked on from first, Jeff stroked the ball hard, and it flew into the outfield. Josh took off like a rabbit, rounded second, and headed for third. The outfielder made a throw to third base, but Josh was safe.

As Alex strode to the plate, Jeff was taking a lead off of first base, and Josh was moving a couple of steps off of third.

Alex gripped the bat and looked over to Stanley for a sign. As Stanley signaled to Alex, both Alex and Josh nodded in understanding.

The first pitch was headed for the outside edge of the plate. Alex began to swing but stopped before the ball arrived as she thought it was too far outside.

The ball smacked into the catcher's mitt, and the umpire called, "Strike."

Deb called from the bleachers. "Come on, Alex, honey."

Stanley clapped and yelled, "OK, Alex. Show 'em what you're made of."

Alex stepped back into the batter's box. As the pitch approached, she moved her bat over the plate and bunted the ball.

As Alex ran for first, the baseball dribbled out between the pitcher and catcher. They both raced for it.

From third base, Josh could see a slight opening. There were already two outs, but the Tigers needed Josh to score to win the game.

She made up her mind.

CHAPTER 29

Stanley looked on from the bench and held his breath. His team desperately needed Josh to score in order to win the game, but there were already two outs, and the Sharks' pitcher deftly scooped up the ball.

Stanley didn't know what he would have done in Josh's place, and he wasn't sure she could make it to home plate, but his heart swelled with pride as she began to run.

The catcher raced back to home plate, and the pitcher skillfully tossed him the ball. As the catcher secured the baseball and moved to block the plate, Josh slid.

Time stood still, and everyone fell silent until the dust settled, and they heard the umpire yell, "Safe!"

The Tigers' side of the bleachers erupted with cheering.

The umpire announced officially, "That's the ballgame, ladies and gentlemen."

The park echoed with cheers, and the bleachers emptied as everyone rushed onto the field.

Stanley scooped up Josh, and they held one another in a tight embrace.

Bernice and the adoptive couple approached Stanley and Josh. Stanley noticed them approaching and set Josh down.

Bernice motioned and called to Josh. "Come on, Josh. We need to be going."

Josh reluctantly complied and began to walk away. She looked back toward Stanley, then stepped alongside the adoptive couple.

Lisa rushed over and intercepted them, giving Josh a big hug. Then Lisa walked over to Stanley and held his hand.

Neither Stanley nor Lisa could speak as they watched Josh leave with Bernice and the adoptive couple.

Stanley squeezed Lisa's hand, trying to encourage her. Then he moved away to congratulate each member of his team and greet all of the parents.

The Tigers and their families, friends, and fans had a great celebration. Stanley and Lisa made a show of joining in, but they both felt empty inside.

That night in the Walters' home, Stanley and Lisa ate dinner silently in the kitchen. As Lisa got up to clear away the dishes, Stanley picked up the lamp and sat gazing at it.

Lisa reached to put away another dish and noticed Stanley.

She asked, "What are you thinking about, Stan?"

She walked over to the table and sat beside him.

Stanley looked at Lisa and said solemnly, "I can't believe she will be gone tomorrow."

Lisa tried to encourage him, saying, "There is nothing you could have done."

Stanley shook his head and admitted, "I could have at least tried, but I was afraid."

Lisa asked, "Of what?"

Stanley sighed deeply and answered. "That in some way, if I were to love *another* child, I would be cheating on Eddy."

Stanley wanted to say more but couldn't put all of his feelings into words.

Lisa spoke encouragingly. "Stanley, honey. I believe you have enough love in your heart to keep what you have for Eddy and to love another child, too."

"But," Stanley argued, "I don't want to love another child. I want to love Josh, and now it's too late."

Lisa and Stanley had a restless night. Stanley got up early and headed for the garage to finish his cleanup project. Lisa and Cooper joined him, and as Stanley was sweeping the floor, Lisa organized the last few boxes and made sure everything was in its place.

As Stanley and Lisa looked at the garage that had been transformed from a mess to an organized space, they were startled to hear a knock at the edge of the garage door.

Stanley and Lisa glanced up and saw Austin standing there.

Austin was nervous and stammered, "Uh, Mr. Walters?"

Stanley nodded. "Yes, Austin. What is it?"

Austin extended his arm, and Stanley could see he was holding Eddy's baseball glove that Stanley had given to Josh.

Austin explained, "This was in Josh's room. I thought you might want it."

Austin handed the glove to Stanley. Stanley gave him half a smile, which was all he could manage.

Stanley muttered, "Thanks."

As Austin turned and walked away, heading back toward Miss Esther's house, Lisa moved toward Stanley. Stanley stood like a statue and silently stared at the baseball glove.

He glanced toward Lisa and then looked down at Cooper who stared back intently. Finally, Stanley sighed, shrugged, and walked over to the box marked *Eddy's Things*. Stanley opened the box and gently placed the glove inside.

As Stanley closed the box, he thought about all the amazing things that had happened since that glove had come out of the box.

Stanley and Lisa looked at one another and then at the box that held the glove. They knew that, for the first time in a long time, the two of them made a family—or at least the two of them and Cooper made a family.

Stanley and Lisa thought about all the things that they had to be thankful for and how far they had come, but they knew there was something still missing.

CHAPTER 30

The Department of Human Services office, which everyone simply called DHS, was a gloomy place where important decisions were made that affected families, children, and their lives.

Inside her office, Bernice Whitcome was sitting at her desk signing a mountain of paperwork. Bernice had gone into the field of social work because she cared about kids, but she often felt like she spent most of her time doing paperwork.

Josh was slumped in a chair across from Bernice's desk. Josh hadn't spoken a word, and she just sat and stared at the floor.

Bernice spoke cheerily. "So, this is the big day. How do you feel?"

Josh couldn't say a word. She had dreamed about being adopted and having a real family for as long as she could remember, but deep down she knew that this was all wrong.

Bernice prodded, "Josh, please talk to me."

Josh looked directly at Bernice and said solemnly, "I want to go back to Miss Esther's."

Josh stared back at the floor as Bernice tried to encourage her. "Josh, this family is very nice, and they want to make this work."

Josh glared at Bernice and blurted, "I don't care. If I can't go back to Miss Esther's, then I don't want to go anywhere."

Bernice looked back down at her paperwork and muttered, "Well, we'll see about that."

Bernice picked up the phone and said, "Alice, can you show them in, please."

Josh stiffened in her chair, folded her arms defiantly, and continued to stare at the floor. Josh heard the door open behind her, but she wasn't going to turn to look at those people. She heard some shuffling behind her, then all was silent.

Josh could barely see something out of the corner of her eye. It was Cooper holding her baseball glove in his mouth.

Josh couldn't believe what she was seeing. It took her a moment to understand what was happening. Then she got a huge smile on her face.

Josh jumped up and yelled, "Cooper!"

She raced over and hugged Cooper around his neck.

Josh glanced up and saw Stanley and Lisa standing in the doorway. She was bewildered and couldn't understand why they were there.

Stanley looked down at her and said, "Hello, Josh."

Josh continued to stare in confusion and asked, "What are you doing here?"

Bernice interjected, "Josh, Mr. and Mrs. Walters are looking to adopt."

Josh looked toward Bernice and then back to Stanley and Lisa. She was trying to make everything fit into place in her mind.

Josh asked, "You guys are here to adopt a kid?"

Lisa walked over to Josh and lovingly answered, "Well, honey, not just any kid."

"Yeah, Josh," Stanley added, "we were wondering if you would consider coming to live with us?"

Josh questioned, "You mean like a foster kid?"

Lisa shook her head and responded, "No. More like a daughter."

Josh stared at them for a moment trying to let it all sink in.

Stanley explained, "There is one thing you will need to consider before you give us your answer."

"What?" Josh asked.

Stanley answered, "You would have to share a room with your sister."

Josh shook her head and declared, "I don't have a sister."

Just then, the door opened, and Bernice's assistant, Alice, walked in with Rachel. When Josh saw Rachel, a huge smile appeared on her face.

Josh exclaimed, "Rachel!" Rachel rushed toward Josh and cried, "Josh!" As the two girls hugged, Rachel dropped her burned rag doll to the floor.

Bernice was overjoyed but feigned an official tone, inquiring, "So, Josh, do you think you might want to live with the Walters after all?"

Josh nodded vigorously, and her eyes shone brightly as she announced, "Yes! I really want to live with them."

Bernice returned Josh's smile and said, "I thought you might change your mind."

Everyone laughed with joy, and Bernice continued. "OK, girls. I need you to go with Miss Alice while Mr. and Mrs. Walters and I talk some more."

Josh was overjoyed. She said, "OK," and started to head toward the door with Rachel; but then she stopped and rushed back to Stanley and Lisa who stooped down and reached out to her. The three of them embraced.

Josh whispered into Stanley's ear, "Thank you for believing in me."

Stanley lovingly responded, "No, Josh. Thank you for believing in me."

Josh walked back to Rachel, and the two girls left the office hand in hand and followed Alice down the hall.

Lisa turned to Bernice and said, "Thank you for all you have done."

"Don't thank me," Bernice explained. "When the Singletons saw you two at the game, they knew you had to be together."

Stanley spoke exuberantly, "It's amazing how this has all worked out."

Bernice glanced down at her desk and said, "Yes, well, I have some papers you will need to sign, and then we can move ahead on these adoptions."

Stanley leaned over Bernice's desk to look at some paperwork she was showing him.

Lisa spotted Rachel's rag doll lying abandoned on the floor. As she picked it up, she spoke knowingly. "She won't need this anymore."

CHAPTER 31

The excitement of the newly formed family was over-whelming in Stanley and Lisa's house. It took several weeks for everything to even begin to settle down in the Walters' home and in the neighborhood.

Stanley and Lisa had gained two new daughters, but Miss Esther felt as if she had gained something, too. She didn't feel as if she had lost Josh and Rachel as they were just next door, and they would be there from now on.

Esther loved kids but could never get fully and totally attached because she understood that, sooner or later, all of her foster kids would move on. It was exciting for her to see Josh and Rachel planted somewhere that they could grow and bloom.

Miss Esther was sitting on her front porch in her rocking chair watching everyone playing next door in the Walters' yard.

Stanley was the proud father enjoying the beautiful day with his new daughters, Josh and Rachel. Alex, Cody, and Austin had joined them in a spirited game of catch.

As Esther rocked silently, taking in the whole scene, Charles and Sam stepped up beside her. They seemed to have appeared from nowhere.

Miss Esther spoke to them as if greeting old friends. "Hello, Charles and Sam. I was wondering when you would visit."

Sam nodded, and Charles bowed and then glanced toward the Walters' yard as he responded. "Just checking in on our girl."

Charles and Esther smiled warmly as they watched Rachel playing contentedly with Cooper.

Miss Esther announced, "I think she is going to be just fine."

As Esther looked back toward Charles and Sam, they had disappeared as suddenly as they had arrived. Esther smiled to herself, knowing they would never be too far away.

Lisa opened her front door and stepped onto the porch carrying a tray with a pitcher of lemonade and cups on it.

She turned toward Rachel and said, "Rachel, honey. Can you go get the ice in the kitchen, and bring it out?"

Rachel sounded cheerful and confident as she spoke in a voice Lisa would never tire of hearing. "Sure, Mom."

As the game of catch raged on in the front yard, Rachel bounded up the porch steps and rushed into the house, heading for the kitchen.

Rachel paused in the living room when she caught sight of the lamp sitting on a table. She smiled knowingly and turned the lamp so she could read the engraved inscription. The lamp seemed to glow from within.

More than anyone, Rachel knew that anything was possible if you could just believe.

About the Author

Jim Stovall is the author of 15 previous books including the best seller *The Ultimate Gift* which is now a major motion picture from 20th Century Fox, starring James Garner, Brian Dennehy, and Abigail Breslin.

He is among the most sought-after motivational and platform speakers anywhere. Despite failing eyesight and eventual blindness, Jim Stovall has been a national champion Olympic weightlifter, a successful investment broker, and an entrepreneur. He is the founder and president of the Narrative Television Network, which makes movies and television accessible for America's 13 million blind and visually impaired people and their families. NTN's program guide and samples of its broadcast and cable network programming are available at www.NarrativeTV.com.

The Narrative Television Network has received an Emmy Award and an International Film and Video Award among its many industry honors.

Jim Stovall joined the ranks of Walt Disney, Orson Welles, and four U.S. presidents when he was selected as one of the Ten Outstanding Young Americans by the U.S. Junior Chamber of Commerce. He has appeared on Good Morning America and CNN, and has been featured in *Reader's Digest*, *TV Guide*, and *Time* magazines. The President's Committee on Equal Opportunity selected Jim Stovall as the Entrepreneur of the Year. In June 2000, Jim Stovall joined President Jimmy Carter, Nancy Reagan, and Mother Teresa when he received the International Humanitarian Award.

Jim Stovall can be reached at 918-627-1000 and Jim@JimStovall.com.

DESTINY IMAGE PUBLISHERS, INC.

VISIT OUR NEW SITE HOME AT
WWW.DESTINYIMAGE.COM

FREE SUBSCRIPTION TO DI NEWSLETTER

Receive free unpublished articles by top DI authors, exclusive
discounts, and free downloads from our best and newest books.
Visit www.destinyimage.com to subscribe.

Write to: Destiny Image
             P.O. Box 310
             Shippensburg, PA 17257-0310

Call: 1-800-722-6774

Email: orders@destinyimage.com

For a complete list of our titles or to place an order
online, visit www.destinyimage.com.

FIND US ON FACEBOOK OR FOLLOW US ON TWITTER.

www.facebook.com/destinyimage   facebook
www.twitter.com/destinyimage   twitter